Jack wanted to kiss her

Eve saw it in the intensity of his look. And she wanted to kiss him back. Badly. So when the elevator doors opened, Eve tugged him inside. Jack caught on quickly, wrapping his arms around her and nuzzling the side of her neck as his erection nudged her thigh.

"Where do we go from here, Eve?" he asked, his breath hot on her skin.

"Wherever we want, Jack."

Then, suddenly, *desperately,* as if a dam had been released, her hands were in his hair, their lips fused, their hips together. She strained closer, grinding her mouth against his, waging a war with her tongue. Somewhere along the way, this had changed from a sexy, flirtatious encounter into a moment of consuming need. Eve ached for him to fill her, to satisfy this craving.

"Jack, where's a condom?" she said huskily, breaking the kiss.

He pulled a foil packet out of his wallet, and Eve quickly plucked it from his fingers, tearing the cellophane with her teeth.

"Unzip your pants. You promised me short and to the point."

Jack took the condom from her and gave her a grin that stole her breath away. "Honey," he said, shaking his head, "I offered brief. But *never* short."

Dear Reader,

In times of stress, or even great joy, I often turn to comfort food. And unfortunately for me, that means chocolate. Sure, I like apples, carrots and celery sticks, but they don't cut it when you need a pick-me-up. Give me Godiva any day of the week. And if I'm trying for semihealthy, I don't mind if the manufacturers stick a piece of fruit or a nut in there, as long as they cover it with rich, dark chocolate.

Eve Carmichael—intelligent, strong, independent, driven—shares my weakness. According to Eve, *nothing* is better than chocolate. Of course, under the right circumstances, this opinion is subject to change. And Eve's corporate rival Jack LaRoux is a tall, dark and dangerous one-man circumstance waiting to happen....

So sit back and enjoy watching Jack convince Eve that some things are, indeed, better than chocolate....

I'd love to hear from you. You can write me at P.O. Box 289, Hiram, GA 30141.

Enjoy,

Jennifer LaBrecque

P.S. I'd highly recommend a little chocolate....

Books by Jennifer LaBrecque

JENNIFER LaBRECQUE

BETTER THAN CHOCOLATE...

HARLEQUIN®

TORONTO • NEW YORK • LONDON
AMSTERDAM • PARIS • SYDNEY • HAMBURG
STOCKHOLM • ATHENS • TOKYO • MILAN • MADRID
PRAGUE • WARSAW • BUDAPEST • AUCKLAND

To Brenda Chin, for your seemingly infinite patience, keen eye and insight, and unfailing encouragement.

ISBN 0-373-69192-0

BETTER THAN CHOCOLATE...

Copyright © 2004 by Jennifer LaBrecque.

This edition published by arrangement with Harlequin Books S.A.

www.eHarlequin.com

Printed in U.S.A.

1

"JACK LAROUX with his pants off. Now there's an interesting thought. I've heard he's yumm-o," Andrea Scarpini declared from her end of the park bench.

"That's definitely not what I meant when I said I'd beat the pants off LaRoux." Eve Carmichael laughed, tilting her head back to soak up the early-spring sun filtering through Manhattan high-rises. Although, it *was* an interesting thought, and one she'd entertained fairly frequently. Eve was pretty sure it meant she needed a life outside of work. But she had no intention of sharing that tidbit with Andrea. "And I don't care if he's *yumm-o* or Quasimodo, I'll beat him fair and square with sheer talent."

"And what if our boy Jack doesn't play fair? He didn't earn the nickname Jack the Ripper by being a nice guy," Andrea said.

Rumors had circulated about Jack LaRoux, Eve's counterpart at Hendley and Wells Advertising San Francisco office in the six months he'd been onboard. Descriptions had included arrogant, extremely talented and ruthless. Oh yeah, and yumm-o. Nice, however, never entered the picture.

Eve quirked her brow at Andrea and opened her bottled water.

"Uh, nice doesn't come into it, does it?" Andrea said. Arguably one of the best graphic artists in the city, Andrea abhorred the high-stakes competitive nature of Eve's job. "I mean they don't call you Eve the Avenger because *you're* nice."

Eve bit back a smile. No, they didn't. She'd earned that nickname ostensibly because she never let anything get the best of her. No one crossed her unscathed. Besides, it had a nice cadence to it.

Meanwhile, Andrea was talking herself into another one of her infamous corners. "I mean, I think you're nice because you're my friend, but not everyone..." She trailed off, squirming on her end of the bench. "You know what I mean."

Eve relented and laughed, tugging Andrea out of the corner she'd backed herself into. "I do know what you mean. It's okay. Do you know what you call a nice account executive?" She took a long swallow of water.

"What?"

"Unemployed."

Andrea wrinkled her nose. "Very funny."

"Nah. Just sorta funny. But listen, it gets even better. I got an e-mail from Kirk Hendley this morning. Whoever wins the Bradley account gets the marketing vice presidency over both the New York and San Francisco offices."

"So, your professional fate rests on farm equipment and lawn mowers?"

"Not terribly glamorous, is it? Lucky for me, I've got one of the best teams in the business working with me." She grinned across the space at her friend and team graphic artist.

Andrea nodded at the compliment. "So, if Jack won he'd have to move to New York?"

"Yes. But Jack doesn't need to worry about moving. I'm going to show him just what our New York office is made of."

"It's only fair to warn you there's already a pool going in the art department whether you or LaRoux will get the job," Andrea said.

Neither the pool nor the fact that a confidential memo she'd seen only three hours ago had already leaked surprised Eve. Office gossip was the local pastime at Hendley and Wells. "Who's the favored winner?"

She took another swallow of water and closed her eyes briefly, reveling in the warmth of the sun on her face and the cool sweetness of the water sliding down her throat. She was only mildly interested in the art department's predictions about who would win the vice presidency. She knew she would.

"The bets are running close to even," Andrea said. Eve opened her eyes and leveled a stare. Andrea couldn't lie worth anything. Flustered, Andrea caved. "Oh, what the heck. Okay, LaRoux's favored two to one because he's a man and Bill Bradley has a reputation for being a good old boy. And because, farm equipment is, well, man stuff."

Eve threw back her head and laughed, earning a dirty look from the couple one bench over. "Man stuff? Jack LaRoux lives in San Francisco. Unless he's some off-the-farm prodigy, he's probably never been any closer to a tractor than I have. Consider this an insider tip. Put your money on me, 'cause I'm going to win." Eve wanted that vice presidency so bad she could taste it. Correction. She didn't want it, she needed it. Maybe *that* meant she needed to get a life, but it was the bottom line—this promotion meant everything to her. "I don't expect Jack the Ripper to play nice. And if he wants to step outside of fair, I'm more than willing to take him on there as well."

"I think it's kind of sick and weird that Kirk Hendley's dangling this vice presidency over your heads like a carrot, making you and Jack compete against each other for it," Andrea said.

"Seems like good business sense to me," Eve countered. "We've both got outstanding track records...." That was no boasting, just fact. "And we'll both turn ourselves inside out to come up with something awesome. Kirk and the client wind up with a kick-butt campaign and one of us winds up with a vice presidency. It's beautifully logical. Guess that makes me sick and weird too."

"Nah. You were that way before now," Andrea teased. Then she sobered. "But what if you lose, Eve?"

"I won't."

"Our team is good, but so is his. What if—"

"Losing is not an option." As a middle kid with an older and younger brother, Eve had discovered at a young age that absolute conviction was the necessary ingredient to winning whatever you wanted, be it an ice-cream cone or a vice presidency. And as a girl, she'd learned to try even harder.

Eve also possessed a perverse streak. The more someone told her she couldn't or shouldn't want something, the more determined she was to get it. Her parents, much as she loved them, had sought to quell her ambition from an early age. As their only daughter, it was okay for her to marry an "ad man" but certainly never aspire to be one.

"You know, you're a little scary when you get that look in your eye." Andrea held her hands up in surrender. "Okay, so, you're going to win. When does the battle commence? Monday? Where's the preliminary meeting? Here in New York or San Francisco?"

"Neither. We're meeting on Bradley's home field— Chicago. Technically, we're both supposed to arrive Monday morning and meet that afternoon. I checked with the travel agency as soon as I got the memo." She smiled. "That's why I rebooked my flight for Friday night after work. Who's to say I can't enjoy a weekend of rest and relaxation on my own dollar?" Eve opened the plastic lid on her salad and squeezed a lemon half over the green leaves.

"And get a jump on the competition?" Andrea asked, unwrapping her steak-and-cheese hoagie.

"Maybe. I might pick up a few things during my weekend of R and R." Namely a competitive edge. She was always on her game with a good eight hours of sleep behind her.

Pencil-thin Andrea looked from her hoagie to Eve's

pathetic excuse for a salad. "How can you eat that?" she asked, biting into her sandwich.

The scent of warm onions wafted over to torment Eve. For a second she fantasized about taking a bite of the juicy steak, melted cheese, grilled peppers and onions on a warm, crisp roll. Instead she stabbed her fork into the crunchy green leaves in her salad bowl.

It was a good thing she and Andrea were close friends, otherwise she'd have to hate the waiflike creature scarfing down the sandwich next to her. Eve tugged at her skirt's too-tight waistband. "I had three choices. Eat the salad and lose weight, buy a new wardrobe or go naked. The first option struck me as the best plan."

"Perry and Godiva?" Andrea asked.

"Yep. Insult to injury. Some women might've lost weight. Not me. I find my boyfriend diddling my secretary on my desk and I binge on Godiva, gain five pounds and wind up with a zit the size of Delaware on my forehead."

"More the size of Rhode Island and it's gone. And you're working on the five pounds. But Perry definitely wasn't worth it."

"Perry's a rat bastard," Eve said without vehemence. She still didn't want to talk about the Perry debacle, even with her best friend. Not because she was brokenhearted. No, it was just so damn embarrassing.

And tawdry. Eve's bare-assed boyfriend and her bare-breasted secretary going at it on Eve's desk. *Her desk.* Ugh. Perry, the cheapskate, couldn't even shell out the bucks for a motel room. Eve had needed an entire canister of antibacterial wipes before she'd felt comfortable sitting at her desk again.

Clearly they hadn't expected her to miss her flight and return to the office. Delores had still been gasping for air and Perry searching for a lie when Eve had calmly picked up their clothes—Perry's carefully draped Armani suit and Delores's size-two skirt— from her guest chair and walked back out the door.

Perry had screamed bloody murder but hadn't followed her down the hall. Too many people worked late for him to give chase with his johnson catching wind. And Eve would bet they were also pretty surprised when security showed up shortly thereafter based on an anonymous tip. Perry had called the next day, not to apologize but to demand his suit back. She'd referred him to the Goodwill she'd passed on the way home.

Getting mad was a waste of energy. But getting even was definitely satisfying.

"He could've told me he wanted to see Delores. It was the deception that bothered me." She tugged at the waistband of her skirt. It wasn't a size two. It was a twelve and it was tight. Too tight.

"Sorry, babe. He was doing more than *seeing* her. Delores is a skinny tramp," Andrea said. Andrea was a good friend.

"Bimbo."

"Floozy."

Eve basked in the satisfaction of name-calling for a few seconds. It was almost as satisfying as a steak-

and-cheese hoagie. Well, not really, but it'd have to do.

"Delores might've been a bimbo, but she was a great secretary. I definitely miss her more than I miss Perry." Eve was still getting used to LaTonya, Delores's replacement.

"You know the whole thing's turned you into something of a legend. The women revere you and the men fear you. Eve the Avenger, superhero to women around the world."

Eve indulged in a little eye-rolling. "I hope they write better copy for the Bradley ad." She tried to bring the conversation back to her latest assignment. Perry was old news. *Embarrassing* old news.

"Hey, they can only work with the material they're given." Andrea tore open the wrapping on a Twinkies. "You ought to have a little weekend fling while you're there. You know, clear out Perry's bad karma."

"I'm not a fling kind of gal. And Perry didn't leave any karma *there*." Things hadn't progressed beyond a few dinner dates and a couple of lukewarm kisses. Despite the surprise element, she'd kept her wits about her and was able to size things up when she'd caught Perry naked. Unless he was extremely good at making the most of what he had, she hadn't missed much.

"There's a first time for everything."

"But—"

Andrea held up her hand, interrupting Eve's rebuttal. Eve shut up. No one in their right mind talked to Andrea's hand. "Eve, you are a genius at work. But you're lousy at picking men. Do yourself a favor. Have a fling."

Eve had Godiva'd her way to the same conclusion—not the fling part, but the bad choice in men. Chocolate hadn't helped and she didn't see that Andrea's advice would, either. "Is a fling going to improve my lousy judgment?"

"No. I personally think you pick those guys to avoid commitment. They're losers, so it's a good reason to dump them. You know, like in *Moonstruck* when Cher tells Nic Cage he's a wolf who'd rather gnaw off his own leg than get caught in a trap."

Eve knew the scene well since she and Andrea had seen the movie about a dozen times since they'd been friends. Andrea had serious Nic Cage fever.

"I do not deliberately pick losers in order to avoid serious relationships." She didn't, did she? That would be seriously warped. "So, tell me again why I should hop into bed with a stranger this weekend?"

Andrea wore a dreamy expression. "Think 'Strangers in the Night,'" she sang the title to the Frank Sinatra classic. Andrea, who'd grown up in Brooklyn, with her grandmother sharing her parents' house, had been weaned on Sinatra, Nat King Cole and Ella Fitzgerald. Andrea was a quixotic mixture of uptown sophisticate and romantic neighborhood girl, virgin extraordinaire still waiting on a man with an equally romantic soul. They, however, were in short supply. "Think romance. It would be fun."

"The only fun I'm interested in is winning that promotion and beating LaRoux."

"I'm just interested in who winds up on top," Andrea said, a teasing glint in her eye.

JACK LAROUX LEANED against the hotel's black marble counter, impatience lurking behind his nonchalance. He needed a swim, a shower and a Scotch. Not necessarily in that order. All three were a mere check-in away.

According to Neville, Jack also needed to get laid. But then again, his assistant considered sex of tantamount importance ninety-nine percent of the time. From day one Jack's perpetual reserve had never inhibited Neville's outrageous tongue.

While he waited on his key card, Jack checked out the bar tucked into a corner on the first floor, visible from the lobby mezzanine. Not crowded yet. Not surprising at seven forty-five on a Friday night. He could probably pick up a Scotch and Neville's prescribed lay in the bar. If that was what he'd wanted. Instead, he'd order the Scotch poolside after his swim.

"Here you are, Mr. LaRoux," said the desk clerk. Meg, according to her name tag, offered a smooth, professional smile along with his key card. "You're in Suite four-fourteen. Is there anything else I can help you with? Do you need a hand with your bag?"

"I can handle it." He picked up the garment bag and the black leather attaché housing his laptop, compliments of Hendley and Wells, and smiled across the desk at her. "Thanks, Meg."

Meg blushed and tucked her hair behind one ear, flustered. Who was he to question why women responded to his smile that way? But they did, and it made his life much easier. Most of the time. "Enjoy your stay, Mr. LaRoux."

"Thanks." Jack shouldered his bag and headed for the bank of elevators, anxious to dump his things in his room and head to the pool. He had energy to burn and swimming laps inspired some of his best thinking.

He rode the glass-fronted elevator to the third floor. The thick carpet absorbed the sound of his footsteps as he walked down the hall.

His cell phone buzzed. Neville's office extension flashed on the caller ID. Jack flipped it open with one hand. "Hi, Nev."

"You will not believe who just called the office looking for you," Neville announced with typical dramatic flair.

"Don't leave me hanging." Jack keyed open his suite door and padded across the thick carpet. He deposited his laptop on the desk.

"LaTonya Greer." Neville paused for effect.

The redhead he'd met at the art gallery opening last week? No. Her name was Leslie or Laura or maybe it'd been Leanne. It wasn't LaTonya. He crossed the sitting room to the bedroom and hung his garment bag in the closet. "Am I supposed to know LaTonya Greer?"

"Hel-lo. Assistant to Eve the Evil One."

"Hmm. I hope LaTonya Greer doesn't torture her boss with hyperbole."

Neville sniffed on the other end. "You'd better hope

she's not as good at her job as I am. Of course, she couldn't possibly be."

Jack grinned at Neville's pretended effrontery and juggled the cell phone on his shoulder as he shrugged out of his jacket. "No one's as good at their job as you are—hyperbole or otherwise. What did Ms. Greer want with me and what did you tell her?"

"It was some nonsense about confirming information for Monday's meeting. I told her you were in a meeting."

"Good. Anything else?"

"Good. That's it? Don't you wonder what she's up to?"

Neville possessed excellent intuition regarding advertising, but he tended to be a tad dramatic, seeing intrigue where none existed.

Jack shrugged, even though Neville couldn't see it over the phone. "I'm sure you handled it with your usual aplomb."

"I did, thank you. Now, what's on the agenda for tonight?" Neville's voice carried that let-us-digress-to-sex tone.

"After I hang up with you I'm going to check out the pool."

"Laps and a Scotch?" Nev asked with a sigh.

Neville sounded as if Jack might break out knitting needles next. It didn't mean he'd grown boringly predictable, it just meant he'd developed a method that worked. Sipping Scotch after a hard swim sparked his creativity.

"I should be poolside—" he checked his Rolex "—in about ten minutes."

"Swim your laps and then check out the bar. All work and no play makes Jack a very dull boy. Find yourself a playmate for the weekend."

"I'm not into—"

"Then you should be," Neville interrupted. "You've been wound up way too tight lately. Think of it as relaxation therapy. You know, all those endorphins released by good sex. Consider it priming the pump for doing your best work on Monday." Neville was nothing if not tenacious. Arguing with him was a waste of breath.

"Sure, Nev," Jack said.

"You're humoring me." Jack should've gone for a more convincing tone. "I'm dead serious about those endorphins."

"I've been busy." And bored. All the women he met seemed the same.

"Nobody should be *that* busy. Speaking of bitches, when's the Evil Eve blowing in on her broom?"

They'd been speaking of bitches? Not in his conversation. Jack shook his head. "You supplied the itinerary forwarded by the travel agent. She's expected the same time I was supposed to be here, Monday morning."

"I'll want a full report on the Avenger."

Eve the Avenger. Or simply, Evil Eve as Neville preferred. She had a hell of a buzz going, not only in the company but in the industry. He'd studied her most recent projects. She was good, borderline brilliant.

"I'm looking forward to meeting her. I admire her work and respect her reputation." He'd even pictured her a couple of times in his head. Tall, thin, distant, cool. Okay, maybe he even had a bit of a fantasy thing going for her.

"Courting the enemy. That is so Machiavellian," Neville said.

"Not particularly. It's just good business. And I wasn't planning to court her, simply meet her. When I get the new position, she'll be an asset to the team."

When he moved into the vice presidency, he'd welcome her talent. And he *would* win that promotion. He knew he was damn good at what he did. And a vice presidency was the kind of success a man like his father recognized.

Henri LaRoux, with icy disdain, had predicted Jack would fall flat on his face when he left the family business to make his way in the advertising world. Henri hadn't understood Jack's driving need to excel outside of the commercial real estate industry and his family's considerable influence. Jack could hardly wait to throw his visible success in his father's face.

Not only did he want the vice presidency for himself, he wanted it for Neville, also. Neville had worked long and hard, giving up the security at his old firm to follow Jack to Hendley and Wells. It was nearly seven on a Friday night and Nev was still at the office.

"She's good, Jack. I'm not so sure about this one." Nev always got this way on a project, antsy and uncertain. But that was okay. Jack was sure enough for both of them. Nothing, or in this case, no one, was going to stand in the way of that promotion.

"Don't worry, Neville. Beating Eve Carmichael is going to be like taking candy from a baby."

EVE DROPPED her towel onto a lounge chair and walked to the edge of the nearly deserted rooftop pool. A couple sat in the hot tub perched a few steps above the pool. Well, they weren't exactly sitting—it was more as if they were devouring each other. Low lighting cast the tables scattered around the stone patio into shadowed intimacy.

To the left, a small bar stood empty except for the bartender and a cocktail waitress chatting at the counter. The waitress looked at Eve to make sure she was okay. Eve signaled with a small wave. She'd swim first, drink later. Smooth jazz floated from hidden speakers. Despite the glass walls and roof, Eve could almost feel the caress of the night air.

She curled her toes over the cool edge of the tiled pool. Underwater lights illuminated the water. Odd how pools looked different at night.

And thank God, this one was practically deserted. She tucked her hair into a swim cap, a carryover from her high-school swim-team days. She'd rather look funky now than have the chlorine wreck her foil job. Green highlights weren't in vogue, and she was going to be at her absolute mental and physical best come Monday morning.

Leaning forward, she sliced into the warm water.

Ah, heavenly. She flutter-kicked to the surface and rolled to her back. Mmm, she could easily stay this way, buoyed by the water, watching the night sky beyond the glass ceiling, lulled by the sultry saxophone solo.

But that wasn't doing squat for the extra five pounds of Godiva residing on her thighs. Unfortunately, the women in her family not only shared lousy judgment in men, but also had a tendency to carry a few extra pounds. Equally unfortunate, they also tended to eat their way through an emotional crisis— and they weren't stuffing themselves with fresh fruit. No, they preferred rich, dark, *fattening* chocolate. Aunt Nelda's backside, jiggling in sweatpants, flashed through her head.

Ugh. Atonement time. Resigned, she rolled to her stomach and struck out with a breast stroke. After the first couple of laps, the rhythm took over and her mind wandered, thinking of nothing, thinking of everything. Some people sat cross-legged on the floor to reach a meditative state. Eve swam.

Stroke, kick, breathe.

Stroke, kick, breathe.

Pool wall, flip.

Thirty laps later, Eve climbed out of the pool. The hot-tub pair were still going at it—she *didn't* want to know what was going on beneath the swirling water—while the waitress was now engaged in deep conversation with the bartender. For all intents and purposes, she was alone.

She pulled off the rubber swim cap and shook her

head, sending her hair tumbling to her shoulders. She finger-combed it—damp, but mercifully not green.

Eve began to towel herself dry. The thick cotton felt great against her damp skin and wet bathing suit. Warm and soft, almost like a touch. Yowza, it'd obviously been too long since she'd actually been touched if a saxophone, a little starlight and a warm towel affected her this way.

"You missed a spot." A man spoke from the darkened area behind her. The mixture of amusement and sensuality in his baritone voice sent a shiver down her spine.

Eve started and the man stepped out of the shadows.

Holy guacamole.

At a glance he was drop-freaking-dead gorgeous. Slightly above average height, black hair, lean, towel casually draped around his neck, a drink in one hand. He was amused sophistication with a killer smile and her heart slammed against her ribs.

"What?" Well, that was marginally better than *huh* with her mouth hanging open.

"You missed a spot," he repeated, taking another step forward. His brows, dark slashes that angled up at the end, lent him a decidedly wicked, sexy look. He caught the end of her towel between his lean fingers and dabbed it against her bare skin, along her collarbone. Her skin quivered and her breath hitched in her throat. She wasn't sure if she was relieved or disappointed when his fingers didn't brush against her. He dropped the towel and it fell back against her breast.

Eve gathered her wits and laughed. He was self-assured arrogance and she was an idiot. "I bet you come with your very own warning label."

For a second he looked startled, and then he laughed, too, a low, sexy rumble that skittered along her nerve endings and settled into a nice cozy warmth in her stomach. He raised his glass in acknowledgment, his lips quirked into a wry smile. "If I do, I'm unaware of it."

Hmm. She thought he was very much aware of it. How many women had melted, just like her, when he had turned that smile on them? She'd bet most.

She shrugged into a cover-up, slid her feet into her mules and picked up her straw bag. "Thanks for making sure I didn't walk around with a wet spot."

"Would you care to join me for a drink?"

She didn't miss the challenge in his eyes that underscored his invitation. Eve hesitated. Was she going to heed that warning label she'd slapped on him?

She'd made it her personal philosophy to never date any man who looked better than she did, a realistic outlook in her opinion. She wasn't exactly a dog, but she wasn't Angelina Jolie either. Extremely good-looking men and average women weren't a winning combination. She'd seen it before. Not only did other women snipe behind Ms. Average's back that her man could do better, but they were bold. They felt free to hit on a hot guy who was with a not-so-hot chick.

Of course, he'd invited her for a drink, not a date. And quite frankly, Eve had never been able to resist a challenge.

"Sure. Why not? I'd love a drink."

2

THE WOMAN COULD DEFINITELY control her enthusiasm. And she'd definitely captured his interest. Jack found her lush curves at odds with the driving determination that put her through thirty laps in thirty-five minutes. He'd counted.

There had been something terribly sexy about the way she'd pulled off her swim cap and shaken out her hair. Sexy, because she hadn't known she had an audience. And then when she'd begun toweling herself—it'd been time for him to make himself known and gain control of the situation.

His smile had flustered her—just for a moment and then the damnedest thing had happened. She'd put him in his place with a laugh.

He indicated a table close to the bar's muted light. "How about here?"

"This is fine."

He placed his glass on the table and pulled out a chair for her. She took the seat with a murmured thank-you and crossed her legs. Dark nail polish gleamed against the pale length of her toes.

Jack sat next to her and caught the waitress's eye, motioning her over. What would she order? He dismissed Sex on the Beach or Screaming Orgasm. Too obvious. Maybe a white wine or a piña colada with one of those paper umbrellas on the glass's rim.

"Hi. I'm Jasmine. What can I get for you?" the waitress asked.

"Scotch. Neat."

Okay. He was doubly intrigued. A woman who swam marathon laps and drank a real drink.

The waitress turned to him. "Anything for you, sir?"

"A fresh Glenlivet. A short one."

"Both of these on your tab?"

He smiled. "Yes. Thank you, Jasmine."

"No," the woman said at the same time. "Put my drink on a separate bill and I'll sign for it."

He couldn't get a read on her. "But I invited you for a drink."

"And I plan to have a drink with you. But it doesn't mean you're buying." Her teeth gleamed in a pleasant, resolute smile.

"Separate tabs it is then."

Jasmine nodded and looked between Jack and the woman as if sizing up her competition.

"I'll be right back." Jasmine flashed Jack a smile and turned back toward the bar. He recognized her look. He could have more than a drink, if that's what he wanted, when her shift was up. Jasmine was a known, familiar quantity.

He turned back to the woman at his table. Flickering candlelight painted her in sepia tones. Amusement danced in her wide-set eyes. What color were they? It was impossible to tell in the semidarkness. And he really wanted to know.

"You don't even have to try, do you?" She leaned back in her chair, steepling her fingers beneath her chin, watching him.

Women often watched him, but not with this detached amusement as if he were some specimen in a jar. "No. Not really."

"I bet you're lethal when you put effort into it," she said, more speculation than come-on. Which made it even more of a come-on for him.

"I don't know that I've ever really tried." *But maybe I will now.* The thought hung unspoken between them.

She shook her head, her hair brushing the slope of her shoulders. "It's a shame to never reach your true potential. That's what happens to people when things come too easy."

Jasmine returned with their drinks and saved him having to answer. And quite frankly he was at a loss as to how to respond—an unusual state for him.

Jack studied the woman next to him. Not beautiful, but attractive. What was it about her that had gotten under his skin? In a flash, he realized it was her utter lack of coyness. One of the most boring aspects of the women he'd met lately was the studied coyness they adopted—*Cosmo* devotees who'd read that they should drop their head, bite their lips and then glance through lowered lashes up at their targeted man.

He recognized the moves because he skimmed *Cosmo*, along with a host of other magazines, on a regular basis to keep his finger on the consumer pulse.

And because he was a detached observer of life and its participants.

"Can I get you anything else?" Jasmine asked.

"No," they both demurred and, after a moment's hesitation and another glance his way, Jasmine slipped away.

The woman lifted her glass and sipped. She had a wide, generous mouth, perhaps a shade too large, but still quite lovely with plump, full lips.

"Mmm. Very nice."

Jack resisted the urge to lean forward and taste the Scotch on her lips.

Instead he contented himself with a sip from his glass. "There's nothing quite like a good single-malt Scotch, is there?"

"I like it, but it is something of an acquired taste." Her arms gleamed in the candlelight, the muscles still delineated from her earlier swim. She pushed her hair back from her face and a faint whiff of perfume teased from beneath the unmistakable chlorine clinging to her hair and skin.

Jack found it refreshing that the woman didn't attempt to fill the silence with chatter.

He ran his finger along the smooth curve of the glass. "Have you been in Chicago very long?"

"No. I just arrived today. Tonight actually. How about you?"

"Tonight as well. I'm unwinding before a business meeting next week. I'm traveling alone," he volunteered, anticipating she'd reciprocate the information.

"I could tell."

He raised his brow questioningly.

"You haven't glanced over your shoulder even once," she said. "If you were here with someone, you would've checked to see if they'd shown up at some point."

Clever. "Neither have you. So, you're here alone as well?"

She finished her drink. "I'm here on business," she answered. She motioned to Jasmine for her tab.

Did she dispense with everything with that same slight ruthlessness? Swimming laps. Her drink. Him.

Jack realized she was about to leave. And he didn't want her to leave. Not only was he not used to being dismissed, he found her total lack of seduction, well, utterly seductive.

"There's no jealous husband at home to mind if I ask you to join me for a late dinner?"

"And I presume you don't have a wife who would object to you inviting a woman to dinner?"

Once again, she ignored his question and posed one of her own.

"She wouldn't mind at all." He smiled at her start of surprise, delighted he'd finally managed to get one up on her. Then he relented. "I'm not married. Or divorced. Or attached to a significant other." Jasmine arrived with the bills and promptly left. The woman reached for one tab.

What was her name? Where was she from? And what did she look like in the light? She'd piqued his interest and that hadn't happened in a long time. "Would you join me for dinner?"

She hesitated, obviously undecided. Women didn't usually hesitate. It took Jack a second or so to realize the knot in the pit of his stomach was nervousness. He wanted her to say yes quite badly. "I promise I don't bite," he added.

"I'll make a note of that. Actually, I need to shower and change out of this damp suit." She signed her bill and tucked a copy into her bag.

"That's not a problem." In his head, he slowly peeled her suit off, over the curve of her breasts, along the line of her back, past the indent of her waist, beyond her hips, down those luscious legs.

She pushed away from the table. "Give me forty-five minutes."

His usual dates would've demanded an hour and a half. Jack stood when she did. "The restaurant off of the lobby?"

"Yes."

"Forty-five minutes then."

She walked away and Jack realized he didn't even know her name. "Wait."

She turned around.

"What's your name?"

"Eve," she tossed over her shoulder. She didn't ask for his name in return. Actually, she didn't hang around long enough for him to tell her.

Eve?

She'd disappeared into the building and Jack pulled her bar tab into the light, checking the signature line where she'd signed for her drink.

Blue ink and plain, bold script.

Room 325.
Eve Carmichael.

ANDREA WOULD'VE FOUND something more exciting to wear, Eve acknowledged, checking her reflection in the elevator on her way down. But then again, Andrea wouldn't have had to worry about the Monday meeting. Still, Eve should've listened to her friend and tossed in a couple of sexy outfits. Instead, she'd made the best of business casual, ditching the jacket that went with her dress.

At least the sleeveless, short black dress covered her Godiva thighs and showed off her taut arms and legs. Then again, Mr. Gorgeous had already seen her in a swimsuit, and a swim cap no less, and he'd still asked her to dinner. Stranger things could happen.

Eve stepped off the elevator. Her pumps clicked against the polished tile as she crossed the lobby to the restaurant. At least her shoes had a decent heel on them.

The man stood outside the restaurant, one shoulder casually propped against the wall, his legs crossed, his attention focused on a handheld piece of electronic equipment. Polished. Sophisticated. Remote.

He looked almost as good dressed in charcoal-gray slacks and a black silk polo as he had in swim trunks and a towel. Eve's heart stalled a beat and then raced to catch up. *Pull yourself together, girl.* He put on his pants the same way any other man did—he just looked better doing it. Andrea's latest hottie simile came to mind—yumm-o.

"Hello," she said as she approached him.

He glanced up and a slow smile curled his lips. He pocketed his Blackberry. Another workaholic. She had, of course, checked her e-mails before she left her room.

"Eve."

Her name rolled off his tongue and trailed warmth through her like a sip of smooth Scotch. His eyes held hers and the same attraction she'd felt earlier at the pool surged between them again. Was that a hint of relief in his eyes? Had he thought she'd stand him up? Amazing. Women didn't stand up a man like him.

"Have you been waiting long?" she asked.

"Not at all." He paused, his gaze sweeping her. "You're lovely."

His words trailed across her skin and shivered through her.

"Thank you. So are you," she said, tossing the compliment, which was actually an understatement when she considered how gorgeous he was, back at him, determined not to be thrown off balance.

"Thanks." She almost laughed at the surprise that flickered across his face.

"The high-maintenance women you date never tell you that?"

"No. Not in so many words." He slanted his head to one side and looked at her, casual male elegance personified. The light gleamed in his dark hair. "Why do you think I date high-maintenance women?"

In a moment of perfect timing, a couple exited the restaurant and walked past. The woman, a willowy blonde with exquisite makeup, hair and clothes glanced back over her shoulder at him. She obviously hadn't slapped herself together in half an hour.

Neither Eve nor her dinner date missed the fact that the school-of-high-maintenance graduate had checked him out.

Eve arched an amused brow. "Lucky guess."

He shrugged off the woman's interest, a gesture that only confirmed for Eve that it was the norm. "Are *you* high maintenance?"

He had to ask? Please. Eve had a penchant for nice jewelry and lingerie, but aside from that, she bought her clothes and shoes on sale at discount stores. Her lack of interest in Jimmy Choo or Manolo Blahnik appalled Andrea. Eve splurged on the occasional spa visit, but didn't have the time or budget to make it a regular part of her life. "What do you think?"

"Not overtly."

That begged an explanation. She raised a questioning brow.

"You don't impress me as needing a constant stream of adoration to feel good about yourself. But I think you don't suffer fools gladly. I'd say you're a woman who speaks her mind and does exactly as she pleases. And the result is very, very sexy." His voice dropped an octave on the last observation and took her breath with it.

Eve's heart repeated that stop-and-race trick. If he kept this up, she'd begin to believe she was closer to Angelina Jolie than she realized. He had the speaking-her-mind and doing-as-she-pleased parts down pat, but she was, quite frankly, surprised he found it sexy. It intimidated most men. But then again, from what she'd seen thus far, he wasn't most men.

"And you strike me as a man who does what he wants and is used to getting what he wants. And that, too, is very, very sexy."

And it was. Eve wasn't so sure that she particularly liked this man. He was arrogant, far too handsome, and he set her on edge. But she was incredibly attracted to him.

"Perhaps we have more in common than you think, Eve."

Caught up in the intimate way her name rolled off his tongue, it took a moment for his comment to register. There was an implied intimacy, almost a hint that he knew something she didn't. Did she know him? Had she met him before? One of her brothers' college buddies? Someone from last year's national conference? Definitely not. A woman would never forget meeting this man. But something about him struck a chord of recognition.

"Do I know you? Have we met before?"

He shook his head. "We've never met before."

Then why did she have this weird, nagging sense of the familiar? *Aha.* Jack LaRoux.

He reminded her of Jack. Not that she'd ever met Jack, but this man was everything she'd imagined her nemesis to be, possibly because she'd had some antagonistic, sexual fantasy thing going in her head around Jack LaRoux for the past several months. Sex and power were inextricably intertwined, and there was definitely a power struggle going on between her and Jack the Ripper. And she was definitely attracted to this man.

She'd come to Chicago early. Had Jack come early as well? He could have, except Eve had read an e-mail ten minutes ago from LaTonya. Jack had been in a late-afternoon meeting when LaTonya had contacted the San Francisco office earlier. Not even the West Coast Wonder Boy could manage to be in two places at one time.

"Hello. I think you've gone somewhere else," he said

"Sorry. You remind me of someone I know."

Annoyance tightened his face and flashed in his eyes. He quickly masked it with the detached air of urbane amusement he wore so well.

"Ready?" Obviously he didn't like being compared to someone else.

"Yes."

They stepped into the restaurant. A bird-of-paradise display in a large vase dominated the entry. A late-dinner crowd filled two-thirds of the white-linen-draped tables. Nice. Very nice. Minimalist, sophisticated decor. A jazz quartet, tucked into a corner, offered a dinner concert. A handful of couples swayed to the music on the small dance floor.

The maître d' appeared. "Two for dinner?"

"Yes. Do you have something with a view?"

"A table with quite a nice view just opened. This way please."

Eve's companion brushed his fingers against her

arm, ushering her ahead of him in a gesture she'd experienced countless times before. But, unlike all those other times, his warm fingers against her bare flesh set her heart racing. Far from being impersonal, his touch echoed through her. Evocative. Sensual.

The subtle scent of his expensive cologne tantalized her. It was incredible how a mere touch and a whiff of fragrance could so thoroughly entice and arouse.

The maître d' seated them. Framed by the window, the city's skyline and dark sky juxtaposed against the reflection of crisp linens, intimate lighting, and them.

The man across the table studied her.

"You have beautiful eyes. I've spent the last hour wondering what color they were."

"Thank you. You could've asked at the pool."

"It wouldn't have been the same thing," he said. "What would you have told me?"

"Blue-green."

"Ah. That's my point. They're not simply blue-green. They're an amazing blend of crystal blue and translucent green, like a natural spring. Beautiful. Bottomless."

She'd heard before how unusual her eyes were, but never had anyone been so eloquent. It was a line. A really impressive line, but a line nonetheless.

"Do you always have such a way with words?"

"Only when I'm suitably inspired...which is seldom."

He definitely knew how to deliver a compliment. And he was definitely just what the ego-doctor had ordered. She mentally gave Perry the finger.

At least five women had eyed him since they'd entered the restaurant. Eve had once gone out with a guy who'd spent their evening dividing his attention between Eve and all the other women in the room. It had been the date from hell. But this gorgeous man seemed oblivious to anyone but her.

The saxophone's husky notes added a layer to the sensual mood, lending a fantasy quality to the evening.

"Eve?"

She looked at the other major player in her unfolding fantasy. "Hmm?"

"Aren't you interested in my name? Who I am?"

The "Strangers in the Night" refrain came to a screeching halt. *No, no, no.* Not just when her fantasy was cranking up.

Andrea had prescribed a fling. Eve was eight hundred miles from home in a city where she didn't know anyone. Fate had delivered this guy. Who was she to shut the door on opportunity when it knocked?

But why should they pretend to look each other up next week? Why make one more bad decision regarding a guy? Besides, she was on the verge of taking on one of the most important projects in her life. She didn't need complications. She didn't want to exchange phone numbers, then wait on a call that never came. Bottom line, she didn't want a relationship. She wanted a memory. Did she want to know who he was?

"No."

"You can be tough on an ego," he said.

Right. His ego seemed fully intact. "Maybe I don't want to spoil this evening by finding out your name is Bert and you manage a tampon factory in Boise."

"Most domestic tampon production is in Detroit."

She'd been tongue-in-cheek with her example but totally serious in her reluctance to kill the night's fantasy. Had she, in one of those weird cosmic turnarounds, hit the nail on the head? "Are you..."

He smiled. Heat suffused her face and neck as she realized he'd got her.

"No. I just made that up. I'm not from Boise or Detroit, and my name isn't Bert. If you don't want to know who I really am..." He leaned forward and brushed his thumb across the back of her hand. A warm, melting heat flowed through her. "Why don't you give me a name? Who would you like for me to be, Eve?"

If she was going for fantasy, why not just go all out?

"Why don't I call you Jack?"

"JACK IT IS." He managed a neutral expression despite his surprise. Was she playing him for a fool? Had she discovered his identity much the same way he'd stumbled on hers? Had the whole Bert from Boise been a clever ruse to throw him off track? "Can I ask, however, why Jack?"

"It suits you." A hint of animosity shadowed her amazing eyes, but unless she was the world's consummate actress, she really didn't seem to know who he was.

"You said earlier I reminded you of someone. Is his name Jack?"

"As a matter of fact, it is."

Damn. Everyone had a past. Why should it annoy him that Eve's past included another Jack. "Ex-husband? Former lover?"

"Nothing so...intimate." The way her low voice caressed the word knotted his gut. "A co-worker if you will. Actually, a rival."

He was the Jack in her past? Life was stranger than fiction. They'd never met before, yet he reminded her of himself. "I see. I don't want to be your rival this evening," he said on behalf of both Jacks, Jack the Imposter and Jack the Rival. And amazingly he didn't. Certainly, if she had anything business related to divulge, he'd listen. But he found himself fascinated by Eve—the woman and the Avenger.

"Poor choice of words. He's my counterpart."

She could backpedal all evening, but the truth as she saw it lay in her initial response. Ethically, he should speak up and admit his true identity. He'd actually tried to earlier, but she had turned down his offer. And he was much more likely to gain insight into her and her plans if she didn't know who he was. An even more compelling justification for keeping his mouth shut was that Eve wasn't likely to stay for dinner if she knew he was Jack LaRoux. At least not on the terms he wanted her to stay. All told, self-interest far outweighed ethics.

"Counterpart sounds like a much more interesting position than rival," he said.

"Perhaps."

"Oh?"

"A truly interesting position would be to become both." Sensuality threaded her voice.

This was the way he'd seen her, fantasized about her even. She was his equal, yet also his rival, and they were locked in a struggle for domination. Arousal, swift and intense, arrowed through him.

Unfortunately, the waiter arrived for their drink order. Or perhaps it was fortunate, as it gave him a chance to recover his equilibrium.

They ordered coconut prawns and a bottle of wine, sommelier's choice.

Jack wasn't hungry for prawns or anything else on the menu. Dinner had merely been a way to get her to see him again. And that was even before he knew who she was. Eve was the most enigmatic, self-possessed women he'd ever met. His younger sister, Marta, would crucify him as a sexist pig, but the truth was, most of the women he knew couldn't wait to tell him all about themselves. He'd never met a woman more closemouthed—or one he wanted to know about more.

"I'm glad you came," he said.

"Did you really think I wouldn't?"

He shrugged. She hadn't shown overwhelming enthusiasm when he offered the invitation. "I hoped you would."

Skeptical amusement lit her eyes. "Have you *ever* been stood up?"

He smiled. Busted. "No."

"I didn't think so."

"There's a first time for everything."

"Hmm. I can't imagine you have many first experiences left open."

"There's enough." He'd had his fair share of sexual experiences, but he had a feeling making love to Eve would be something truly unique.

"Such as?" she asked.

Probably best not to bring up making love...yet. "I've never been married or engaged. I've never forfeited a handball game." He smiled. "There's a whole range of first experiences waiting for me." *Including you.*

The waiter arrived with the wine. After the obligatory sniff and taste test, he poured two glasses of the pale drink and left.

Eve traced the glass rim with a neat, unpolished nail and picked up their conversational thread. "How about love? Have you ever been in love, Jack?"

Ah, the irresistible topic of love. "No. I've never succumbed to the power of Aphrodite." He paused as she raised the wineglass to her full, generous mouth and sipped. "But then again, Aphrodite's a myth."

"Delicious," she said, complimenting the wine and regarding him over her glass rim. "Love's a myth?" She didn't display feminine outrage, merely amused interest.

"Love's a shadow puppet. People hide their real emotions and motivations behind it. Lust, passion, obsession, manipulation. Cloak them in the guise of love and all's right with the world." For her, for now, he would pretend to be himself, which worked out because he drew the line at pretending to be someone he wasn't.

Eve tucked a loose tendril of hair behind her ear. "It must be difficult."

"What?"

"To view the world through such a dark shade of cynicism," she said, her tone more amused than mocking.

He shrugged. "I manage." He was what he was. "What about you, Eve? Have you ever been in love?"

"No." She didn't hesitate. "But that doesn't mean it doesn't exist."

Unflappable. Composed. She stared at him with those beautiful eyes. "Ah. Are you that delicious garden variety who considers herself one lucky date away from destiny?"

She laughed, a low chuckle that strummed through him. "Perhaps...but not tonight, Jack."

"Touché." And that was good news. Wasn't it?

"What? Aren't you relieved?"

"Absolutely." He didn't buy into that destiny nonsense. But he did believe in the strong attraction sizzling between them. Her emotional distance spurred his desire to hold her close. He held out his hand. "Dance with me."

She put her hand in his and stood. Energy pulsed between them. He led her to the floor and drew her into his arms. She fit perfectly...at least for the night.

Her subtle scent and warm flesh teased him. He glanced into her eyes, crystal-clear pools alight with humor and intelligence, and a touch of mockery. She was warm, fluid, graceful and totally unreachable, even though he held her in his arms.

His intense reaction to Eve surprised him. What was it about her? She wasn't overly beautiful, accomplished, or even particularly well dressed. But the fact remained, he wanted her more than he'd wanted any woman in a long time, perhaps ever. There was the element of the forbidden, the unattainable, about her. Perhaps he wanted her for the same reason she wanted to call a stranger Jack. The thought of this self-possessed woman as a conquest... His cynicism didn't exclude himself and Jack always got what Jack wanted.

The song ended and they returned to the table. During their dance, the waiter had delivered their orders.

"You're quite a good dancer," he said. And she was—with a strong partner. Otherwise she would've slipped into the lead.

"Thanks." Eve forked a plump, succulent shrimp. "My mother insisted all of us have ballroom dance classes. Learning to tango at Arthur Murray Dance Studio qualified as teen torture, but it's paid off. Except I do have a tendency to try and lead...." She smiled and then neatly bit the shrimp in two.

He couldn't contain an answering smile, charmed by her self-assessment. "I noticed."

She grimaced. "I'm sure you did. My instructor used to say dancing with me was more work than pleasure."

His body still held the imprint of her heat, her scent,

her soft curves. "Then he obviously never danced with you once you'd grown up."

She smiled. "I've changed a little bit since I was fourteen. What about you? Where'd you learn to dance like that?"

"It was a required course at boarding school. I got top marks in my class."

He sounded like a desperate adolescent trying to impress the pretty girl who refused to be impressed. He'd witnessed it countless times, but he'd never been in the position himself. Not until now. He didn't relish the role.

"It shows," she said.

"If you're going to do anything, you should do it well. I go for top marks every time." And she'd do well to remember that.

"Everything?" Husky innuendo underscored the challenge.

"Everything."

"My older brother once told me that beautiful girls weren't as good in bed because they felt like it was enough of a treat for the guy to simply be there with them."

Jack laughed, startled by her candor. He'd drawn the same conclusion on more than one occasion. But he'd be damned if he'd ever had a date voice it. Once again, she wrestled the upper hand from him.

"Are you warning me or is that a general observation?"

"Neither. I'm quizzing you. Is that the way it is with

men?'' How did she manage to be so blunt and bold, yet remote? As if he amused her, for the moment.

"I don't know. I've never slept with a beautiful man and I don't intend to start. Not even to satisfy your curiosity." He delighted in misconstruing her meaning.

"There are far better ways to satisfy my curiosity as to whether breathtakingly handsome men try as hard."

Jack's ability to visualize was one of his greatest assets in his job. And right now he could visualize very clearly Eve naked beneath him, her ankles hooked over his shoulders, his hands gripping her thighs, while he proved just how *hard* and thoroughly he could convince her.

"I'm sure I could satisfy...your curiosity. As I said before, I go for top marks in everything."

"Interesting. We do seem to have a lot in common. I, too, have a compulsion to be the best. That's one of the reasons I'm here. To show my competitor that there's only one spot at the top and it's mine."

"Jack? Your rival?"

"Jack."

"So this is business?"

"Monday it's business. This weekend is pleasure."

The way pleasure rolled off her tongue brought out the best of Jack's visualization skills again, arousing more than his intellect.

"You like being on top?" he asked. Instant image— her astride him. Instant erection.

"Absolutely."

"And how do you think Jack will take you being on top?" he asked softly.

She shrugged one nearly bare shoulder. "I'm sure he'll take it like a man." A slow, wicked smile crooked her mouth. "How would you take it, Jack?"

As much as he hated being predictable, he was a man and her provocative choice of words tightened his entire body. "I'd uphold my end of the deal...until I could reverse positions. What if you don't come out on top, Eve? What if Jack gets that spot?"

"He won't."

Jack recognized bluffing when he saw it. Eve wasn't. She spoke with absolute conviction, as if she already owned the equipment account.

He'd seriously miscalculated. When he won the vice presidency, Eve wouldn't be part of his team. Now that he'd actually met her, he knew she'd never work under him. Eve the Avenger was as good as gone.

Which left him free to do what he'd wanted to all evening—kiss her remarkable mouth until her composure shattered to hell and back.

3

JACK WANTED to kiss her. Eve saw it in the intensity of his look. And while she wasn't sure that she particularly liked him, she did want to kiss him. Badly. Actually, she'd like to have her wicked way with him until they were both singing the "Hallelujah Chorus." But the telling would be in the kiss. Sometimes reality simply didn't live up to fantasy's expectations.

She looked for a conversational opener other than, *Would you like to explore how hot things can get between us?* "Would you like a prawn?" she asked.

He pushed his plate away with one finger. His eyes fastened on her mouth. "No. I'm not hungry for the prawns," he said, his voice low and soft.

Anticipation blossomed deep in her belly and pooled between her thighs. She returned the look, letting him see the want that surged through her.

"Are you ready to leave?" he asked.

"Yes."

Jack signaled the waiter, who promptly appeared with the bill. After paying the check, Jack rose to his feet and pulled out Eve's chair. It was a gallant gesture very few men bothered with and something about it struck Eve as sexy. Well, actually, right now, anything short of seeing toilet paper stuck to the bottom of Jack's shoe would probably strike her as sexy.

They wound their way through the tables. His fingers rested at the indent of her waist and seared her through the fabric. His scent, expensive and unmistakably masculine, seduced her.

Her pulse was thundering and she wanted to kiss him quite desperately. And if the look in his eye was a barometer, he felt the same.

Urgency sent them ducking through the first unmarked door outside the restaurant. Jack tugged her into a small hallway behind him. Despite the haze of desire surrounding her, Eve had the presence of mind to notice a service elevator to the left and the muted sounds of the busy kitchen partially contained by a door straight ahead.

Jack turned to Eve and bracketed her shoulders with his hands. "I've wanted to do this since I saw you at the pool."

His head lowered by slow degrees, plenty of time for her to protest or twist away. Instead, she slid her arms around his waist and murmured a breathy yes.

Anticipation coursed through her, heightened her awareness of his hands on her, his scent, the hint of wine clinging to his warm breath as he leaned closer.

His lips settled against hers. Sure. Firm. Commanding. He tasted of warm male and cool, crisp wine. And detachment. There was something very contained about his kiss that she wanted to let loose. She'd seen the heat behind his droll air. She'd felt it rush to fill the space between them, around them, within her.

He lifted his head. His dark gray eyes held a slightly dazed look and Eve reconsidered. Perhaps he wasn't as contained as he seemed.

For a second she questioned the fairness of using this stranger as a fantasy stand-in. Then she dismissed the idea. They were just two strangers in the night. For all she knew, she was his stand-in for someone else as well.

He stroked her arms, featherlight caresses that weighted her limbs with a heated lethargy and chased away all other thought. He rained equally light, teasing kisses along her jaw.

Eve closed her eyes and absorbed the sensations. The faint scrape of his beard. The mingled scents of expensive cologne, professionally laundered clothes, and wine. His warm mouth maddening against her skin, her body alternately tightening and softening with desire.

"Oh, Jack." She plied her fingers along his lean back.

Beneath his silk shirt, his muscles grew taut under her fingertips.

"Eve..." His husky murmur stroked through her.

She pulled him close and nibbled at his mouth with small, sucking kisses. He groaned and plowed his fingers into her hair, wrecking her loose upsweep. Some of his detachment tumbled along with her hair. *Yes. Much better.* Eve smiled her satisfaction around the kisses she delivered.

He molded his fingers against her scalp and ground

her mouth to his for a no-holds-barred, devouring kiss.

Heat flashed through her. Need consumed her—the need to touch and be touched, to simultaneously sate and tempt. She wrapped her leg around his, feeling the hard line of his thigh and his jutting erection pressing against her. He smoothed his hands over her back and cupped her buttocks, pulling her tighter, harder against him. Her breasts strained against the hard wall of his chest. His scent, one she would forever associate with intense, piercing arousal, surrounded her.

In the recesses of rational thought, a ding registered. Barely.

"Excuse me."

Eve and Jack broke apart. A uniformed staff member stood expectantly with a room-service cart. Eve realized she and Jack were blocking his exit. Tugging her dress down, Eve moved aside so the waiter could pass.

Once upon a time, like pre-tonight, she might've been mortified to be caught in a semipublic makeout session. Now she was simply caught up in the throes of heavy-duty lust with no room for embarrassment.

"Sorry about that," she apologized as she moved aside.

"No problem." The blushing waiter trundled past and pushed his cart through the kitchen door.

Jack turned to her. "We should probably find a less public place."

"I know just the spot." Eve hit the call button and tugged him into the elevator with her when it opened.

"Are you claustrophobic?" she asked over her shoulder as she pressed the close button.

"No, I'm not." Jack stepped closer and wrapped his arms around her from behind. Eve pushed the stop button and leaned back into his lean body. He nuzzled the side of her neck and the back of her shoulder, his arousal nudging between her buttocks.

"Mmm." Eve sighed her approval.

"Where do we go from here, Eve?" he asked, his lips never leaving her bare neck.

"Wherever we want it to take us." She turned in his arms to face him. Leaning in close, she let her voice drop to a husky octave. "Where do you want to go, Jack?"

"What destinations are available?"

"Paradise. But it's not a one-way ticket. We can't stay and we'll end up back where we started. But it should be an interesting trip with a few excursions along the way."

"Are you sure you want to offer this trip?" he asked. She saw how much he wanted her, in the harsh lines of his face, the heat in his eyes; felt it in the hard ridge of his arousal, the brush of his lips. Yet he'd offered her the chance to change her mind. It was charming, sweet even, and altogether too romantic for a one-night stand.

"Positive. As long as you realize it's a one-time offer," she said.

"What if I enjoy paradise so much I want to go back?"

"Return fare isn't an option." No way. She wasn't

making another bad man decision. Besides, she was already thinking of a more immediate problem. She had never had a one-nighter and she wasn't sure of safe-sex etiquette. "When visiting a foreign place, safety precautions are a necessity. Are you suitably equipped?"

He offered a wry smile. "I'm ready for travel."

Thank God. "Then what's your room number, Jack?" Going to his room kept her in control of the situation. Then she didn't have to worry about getting him out of *her* room afterward.

"How do you know I'm not Jack the Ripper?"

She started. How did he know LaRoux's nickname? Then she dismissed the notion. Of course he didn't know Jack. It was a standard play on the Jack of infamy.

She got the impression he wasn't used to picking up women for one night either. At least not successfully, given all the opportunities he kept offering her to back out.

"I'm a black belt. I can take care of myself." Her mother had insisted she have every obscure training known to man. As a result, Eve knew a little bit about a lot of things but was a master of none. Technically she was only an orange belt, but he didn't need to know that. He, however, should be more careful picking up strange women. "How do you know I'm not that crazy woman from *Fatal Attraction?*"

"Even if you were, I don't have a wife or a bunny. Besides, a woman who doesn't want my real name isn't likely to stalk me." His warm breath brushed against her neck. And then his mouth was doing the most incredible things to the tip of her earlobe, a nibbling/laving combination that feathered sensation down her spine.

"Oh..." she sighed. She thumbed his flat, male nipples through his shirt and his entire body tightened against hers.

"Eve..."

"Jack, we've got about one minute before someone checks out why this elevator's stopped." She would be mightily bent if this fantasy were interrupted now....

He reached around her and pushed a button, rendering the elevator operational again. "I want more than a minute to satisfy your curiosity." He clasped her hand in his and brought her hand to his lips. His warm breath and firm lips grazed the sensitive flesh of her palm. She shuddered. "You do remember when the topic came up, don't you?"

"Oh, yes." Her hip pressed against him and she laughed, a low husky chuckle she barely recognized as her own. "And it's still up."

"Well, I'm going to try very hard. I think it will probably take more than once. Sometimes brief and to the point is good. Other times a lengthier, more in-depth approach brings greater satisfaction. I think we should try both and see which you prefer."

"I'd like to start with brief and to the point. I'm not sure I have the patience to make it through the longer version. But I do think we need to get to your room."

Jack reached around her and pushed the button for the fourth floor. Finally, they were on their way. Eve buried her fingers in his hair and tugged his mouth down to hers for another melting kiss.

This man, or perhaps it was the circumstances, had stirred a hunger in her that she'd never felt before. Except maybe those fantasies she'd contrived around Jack LaRoux.

The doors slid open and Jack dragged his mouth from hers with flattering reluctance. He kept his arm wrapped firmly around her, his hand intimately branding her hip as they left the elevator. He paused, obviously disoriented. "Oh, yeah. It's this way," he said.

Eve bit back a smile. She'd take a wild guess he'd never used a service elevator before. With his hair askew from her marauding fingers and the fire in his eyes, he wasn't nearly as urbane but he was twice as sexy.

A short walk down the hall, one card swipe and they were in his suite. The door had barely closed before they turned to each other, desperate, as if a dam had released. Her hands were in his hair, their mouths fused, their hips together, his erection thrusting against her. Her nipples stabbed against the hard wall of his chest and she strained closer, grinding her mouth against his, waging a war with her tongue.

Somewhere along the way, this had changed from a pleasant encounter to a consuming need. It was as if every nerve ending had gathered in her breasts and between her legs. She ached for him to fill her, stretch her, satisfy this craving.

Jack hooked his thumbs beneath her straps and slid

them over her shoulders. Her dress slithered down until it was caught between them. With a small laugh, Eve shifted her hips back and the dress fell free. He was good—had obviously had lots of practice. She hadn't even realized he'd unzipped her dress.

She slid her hand into the niche between their hips and stroked him through his trousers. He moved against her. "Eve."

There was something very liberating about getting naked with someone you weren't hell-bent on establishing a relationship with—it was much easier to undress for a stranger who would remain a stranger. The evidence of too much Godiva on her thighs wasn't nearly as inhibiting. And the appreciative heat in his eyes didn't hurt, either—especially considering this was a man who could have his choice of women.

"Jack, where's a condom?"

"In my pocket."

She plied her hand once again along his length. "That's some condom you've got there."

With a short bark of laughter and a searing look of promise, he pulled a foil packet out of his wallet. Eve plucked the packet from his fingers and tore the cellophane with her teeth.

"Unzip your pants. You promised me short and to the point."

He shook his head. "I offered brief, never short," he said as she slid the zipper down.

Eve's burgeoning laughter died in her throat as his erection sprang free. "No, short isn't an issue."

She smoothed the condom over his rigid length. He

pulsed against her fingertips and she leaned forward. Slowly, deliberately, she licked the column of his throat, up past his chin. She pressed an openmouthed kiss against his lips, stroking her tongue along the length of his. His shudder reverberated through her.

He reached between them and his thumb brushed against her, her satin underwear a damp barrier between them. She shook with the need to have him touch her *there*. She moaned.

He wrenched his mouth from hers, his breathing deep and harsh. "Take your panties off, Eve," he ordered. "Please," he tacked on.

Somewhere along the way, they had stumbled across the room to the sofa. Eve slid her underwear off with one hand, her other hand braced on Jack's chest. Then she pushed Jack backward, onto the sofa. Leaning forward, bracing her hands on his shoulders, she straddled him with her legs spread, feeling the rush of cool air against her hot, wet flesh.

It was a good deal like spilling your guts to a stranger on the subway—you could be brutally honest and it didn't matter because you'd never see them again. So, far from feeling inhibited by any lack of intimacy, she found their relative anonymity intoxicating. She was a siren and she'd have her way with him.

"My panties are off, Jack."

His face was mere inches from her own and Eve knew that before she was through with him, she'd know the satisfaction of replacing his arrogance with sharp desire. She'd see him beg. But not now. Now she wanted him too intensely.

He exhaled sharply, his eyes scorching her as they flicked over her.

"I noticed." He cupped her bare bottom and tugged her forward.

She was so ready, so wet and throbbing, the first wave of an orgasm rolled through her as she sank onto his hard length. Actually, she was so ready he could have probably talked her through it. But this was much, much better, she reasoned with a playful smile, as she clenched her muscles around him.

"Eve," Jack panted, burying himself deeper within her. It was fast and hard for both of them, and her orgasm swept through her with the enervating force of a tropical storm, leaving her wet and buffeted.

"Yes, yes, yes." She realized the frantic voice reverberating through the room was her own as she collapsed against Jack's chest.

"Good Lord, woman, let's hope security doesn't show up. You didn't tell me you were a screamer," he teased, his eyelids lowered, his fingers still stroking a lazy rhythm on her behind.

"Mmm." Eve gave a contented sigh and smiled without responding. She'd never, ever let herself go that way. She'd never had a reason to scream before. If she wanted him to ask her out on a date tomorrow or next week, she might've been embarrassed by his teasing. As it was, she was just satisfied.

A delicious lethargy weighted her limbs. She didn't think she could move. A least not until they were both ready again. With that thought, the first stirring of new arousal blossomed inside her and, like a slow simmer, began to build again.

She shifted slightly against him. Maybe she was destined to become a wild woman, sleeping with strangers regularly. Because this experience had been awesome. And that was actually a more comforting thought than the alternative—that this particular man was a fever in her blood.

4

JACK PUSHED a lock of blond hair off Eve's forehead, unsure of what she would do next, only knowing he didn't want her to leave just yet. "I know this is a round-trip ticket, but we both signed on for extra excursions, didn't we?"

He traced his finger along the length of her short, straight nose and smoothed his palm along the flat, almost-Slavic cheekbone that lent her a faintly exotic look.

"Absolutely. The side trips are half the fun," she said, similarly trailing her fingertips along the underside of his jaw, sending a new wave of sensation coursing through him.

Jack bent his head and brushed her lips with his. "Let's move to the bedroom," he suggested.

"Mmm." She smiled, not lifting her head from the sofa. She didn't look particularly ready to move anywhere. But she did look sated, with a faint slumberous glow in her eyes that promised pleasures to come.

"I'd just like a little more room to maneuver on the next trip." And he was ready to lose his clothes and feel her body, skin to skin.

"I'm convinced. I'm just not sure my legs are able to make the trip." Her slow smile took his breath.

"I can take care of that." He was still reeling a bit with orgasmic aftershock, but the need to impress her with his machismo, something he'd never felt compelled to prove before, pushed him to stand. He scooped her up off the sofa.

He paused for a moment to balance her weight and get his land legs. Her face was right below his. Her initial look of surprise was replaced with a carnal appreciation. So, Miss I-Want-To-Be-On-Top liked being carried into the bedroom. What other fantasies lurked behind those beautiful eyes?

"You know that if you drop me, it's going to screw this romantic scenario up." Her voice, rich with laughter and seduction, resonated against his chest.

"You mean that if I drop you, the trip is over?"

"Pretty much." Her eyes danced. "Especially if you put out your back...or more."

Whoever knew that a sense of humor could be so incredibly sexy?

"I won't drop you." He pretended to stagger—which was only partial pretense. She was heavier than she looked. Must be all that toned muscle. She wasn't kidding about the black-belt thing.

He shouldered open the bedroom door and crossed the room. He lowered her onto the king-size bed and she sank into the thick, down comforter.

Jack paused, one knee braced on the mattress edge, enjoying the view. She wore a black, plunging bra, stiletto pumps and a lot of bare skin in between. "You are gorgeous."

Not particularly original on his part, but heart-thumpingly true.

Smiling, she rose to her knees, and reached behind her to unhook her bra. "And you're overdressed. Take your clothes off, Jack," she said.

Jack was no stranger to naked women. Many wore their nudity with a curious vulnerability. Not Eve. She finished undressing with a sensual lack of self-consciousness he found incredibly arousing.

"Give me just a minute and I'll gladly oblige," he promised with a smile. He popped into the bathroom and rummaged through his shaving kit for another condom. Eve was waiting on the bed in a sexy sprawl.

A momentary pang of guilt speared him. The woman in his bed thought she was indulging in a fantasy with a stranger. But Jack *knew* he was sleeping with Eve Carmichael. But what the hell? She thought he was the stranger that she wanted him to be anyway.

He shrugged off his conscience along with his shirt, enjoying the appreciative heat flickering in her eyes. He stepped out of his shoes and pulled off his socks. She rose to her knees to get a better look. So, without turning away, he stepped out of his trousers and shed his briefs.

She looked him over, her appreciation apparent in the smile that curved her full mouth. "That's much, much better."

He approached the bed without joining her there. Instead, reaching forward, he cupped her head in his hands, drawing her to him. He slid his hands down the satin smoothness of her neck until his thumbs found the hollow indents of her collarbone.

"That brief trip was just a preview. Now I want the whole journey with you." Eve's pulse pounded, beckoning beneath his fingertips. "I want to satisfy every inch of your curiosity. I want to feel the slide of your skin against mine." He skimmed his hands over her shoulders, along the soft down of her arms, past her delicate wrists, capturing her hands in his.

Jack was used to watching. He watched people and their reactions; he watched situations and read them—all with a certain measure of detachment. But now he was fully engaged, caught up in absorbing her scent, her touch, her essence. He, ever the seducer, found himself fully, finally seduced.

"I think I can accommodate that request." Eve's slow smile and husky-voiced acquiescence simmered through him. She ran her hands over his shoulders and pulled him closer until her nipples teased his chest, her belly pressed against his, her smooth thighs embraced his hair-roughened thighs, and her honey-eyed mound cradled his penis.

He buried his fingers in the luxury of her hair and bracketed her head. "Ah, Eve," he murmured. Entreaty. Accolade.

Her kiss demanded as much as it gave. Teased. Tormented. And still he felt no closer to the true essence of the woman who had fascinated him from the first moment he saw her.

He dipped his head lower and captured her nipple in his mouth. Her shudder echoed through him. She arched back, thrusting her turgid point deeper into his mouth. He braced her with his hands behind her back, while he sampled first one breast, then the other.

"Oh, Jack." Her cry of pleasure reverberated against him. He laved the delicate points as if they were succulent berries. He trailed his hands down the satin length of her back, the indent of her waist, the luscious curve of her hips, the rounded mound of her buttocks, the sweet juncture of her bottom and thighs, tracing the honeyed folds between her legs. Her apparent lust fueled his own and need raged through him.

He found the nub of her desire and swept his finger against her. She gasped and arched into him.

Unable to hold out any longer, he smoothed on the condom and lowered her to her back. Playing out his earlier fantasy, he raised her ankles to his shoulders, opening her to his gaze, twisting the knot of lust inside him even tighter. "Are you ready? Is this what you want?" His own voice, thick with desire, sounded alien to him.

"Yes." Her throaty response was enough. He grasped her thighs and entered her in one smooth stroke. Time was suspended as they both became still. She pulsed around him and he quivered in response. One more thrust and he was as deep as he could go.

In one smooth, long stroke he pulled almost all the way out, until they both wanted to protest against the absence of the other. Jack fought the urge to pump faster and harder, holding them in check with slow, smooth strokes that built in intensity, fueling the fire between them. It would have been so easy to bring them both to another quick and ready orgasm, but it was too soon.

He waited until he saw the tight lines on Eve's face and felt her clenching him harder on each stroke. He waited until he was one stroke away from exploding inside her and then he pulled out.

"Jack." Despite her glittering eyes and ragged breath, she was still far too much in control.

He rolled her nipples between his fingers. "Not yet. Don't be so impatient."

A smile of wicked intent replaced her frown of frustration. "This a game of endurance?" She slid her feet down off his shoulders and along his chest. "Didn't I tell you I always play to win?"

She gave a low, sexy laugh, then did something with her feet and suddenly, Jack found himself sprawled on his back. In an instant she was astride him, her wet heat tantalizingly out of reach of his jutting erection. She leaned forward and trailed kisses along his neck, his chest—the brush of her hair and nipples against his skin as enticing as the feel of her mouth.

He gasped as she slid lower down his body and the soft mounds of her breasts cradled his hardness. She delivered mind-blowing, sucking kisses to his belly while she rolled his nipples between her fingers.

"Mmm," Eve murmured, the same way someone savors a particularly tasty treat.

"Oh...Eve..." He trailed off and gave himself up to the pleasures of the moment.

She filled his senses—her scent, her low sounds of approval, the taste of her lips and skin that lingered against his own, the feel of her against him, the sight of her slowly unhinging him kiss by intimate kiss.

She looked up at him, her hair a sexy tangle, her breasts sliding against his erection. "I am so hot for you. Do you want to know how hot?"

Only with every quivering, enflamed, desperate-for-her fiber of his being. "Yes. Show me," he managed to say.

She rose up and slowly impaled herself on him, instantly sending him into her tight, wet heat. She stilled and Jack felt the control she exerted to keep herself from coming. It was the same will he was employing.

"That feels so good, doesn't it?" she said.

"Yes."

"And this feels even better doesn't it?" she asked, sliding up and down his shaft in slow, deliberate strokes. Then she stopped.

He hadn't thought he could get any harder. Now he knew better. "Please...don't stop."

She let out another wickedly sexy laugh and moved over him again, setting a leisurely, measured pace. Jack closed his eyes and lost himself in the sensation. But as good as it felt, it wasn't enough. He grasped her by the hips and urged her on, thrusting against her.

"Tell me what you want," Eve ordered in a hot, breathy voice.

He was beyond murmuring sweet nothings and he didn't think she'd appreciate them anyway. Jack relayed in blunt, no uncertain terms what he wanted and how he wanted it. Far from embarrassing her, it seemed to further excite her.

There was nothing sweet or gentle as she rode him hard and fast, her breasts keeping their own erotic rhythm. It was hot and sexy and he tightened in anticipation of the release that hovered just out of reach. He was almost there and so was she. They...were... so...close....

Then she stopped. Or to be more exact, she slid off of him, leaving him throbbing. Eve had just given him a first. He now knew the thin line that separated intense pleasure from pain.

"Eve..." He pulled her down beside him.

She cupped him in her hand and squeezed, "Think how good it will feel when we both come," she murmured into his mouth.

God, he wanted her, not just the release, but her, more than almost anything he'd ever wanted in his life. He devoured her with his mouth and hands and she strained back, consuming him equally.

She threw her leg over his and urged him inside her. He didn't need a second invitation. It wasn't the optimal position, but they were so hot for each other, so poised on the brink that with one thrust she began to shudder from the waves he felt radiating from inside her.

"Who am I, Eve?" She'd hate him for this later. Really hate him, but he needed to hear it, had to hear that it was *him* that had her so hot, so ready, so unglued.

"Jack," she gasped as another shudder ran through her.

The surge of her orgasm unleashed his, which rolled through him like a firestorm, fierce and unstoppable.

Spent and sated, Jack's limbs refused to move but his mind was racing ahead, almost as if his incredible orgasm had released an endorphin surfeit. When Eve discovered he really was Jack LaRoux, he hoped she didn't black-belt kick his ass. Considering the sexy way she'd flipped him to his back and straddled him, it was a very real possibility. And one he feared a lot less than not being able to find himself in her again.

"DO YOU NEED the bathroom?" Jack asked, pausing at the mattress's edge.

"No. I'm fine. Thanks," she said. He really was very thoughtful and Eve was doubly glad she wouldn't get to know him better. She didn't have to worry about Jack entertaining her secretary on her desktop. Better to lament the fantasy of the one that got away than consider it a lucky escape at the end of a relationship. Disillusion stank—on ice.

Eve stretched on the rumpled bedcover and watched Jack's well-formed backside disappear through the bathroom door. He had the long, lean body of a runner or a swimmer. She smiled at nothing in particular—in fact, she couldn't seem to stop smiling. That had been one awesome version of the "Hallelujah Chorus" and she had personally hit a few unprecedented high notes.

She silently congratulated herself. She was finally showing good guy judgment. She wasn't emotionally vulnerable. She might've stripped off all of her clothes, but she wasn't laying herself naked to another man ever again. Instead, she was experiencing fabulous sex with a lover who was as into her pleasure as much as his own. And, an added bonus, she could walk into that meeting on Monday morning without falling prey to sexual fantasies about Jack LaRoux. After all, she'd *had* him all weekend. This fling business was the way to go.

Jack walked back into the room, a towel slung low around his lean hips. Eve smiled at his modesty. And rather than feed her own self-consciousness, it accentuated her pleasure in her own nudity.

She slid off the bed and crossed to the bathroom. She avoided the mirror, opting instead to cling to the image of herself as a seductress. In record time, she returned to the bedroom, her breath catching in her throat at the sight of the towel-draped man lying on the rumpled down comforter.

The air held the arousing scent of their earlier lovemaking. Eve crossed the room, the quiet broken only by the air conditioner's faint hum.

She'd attributed the towel he wore to modesty earlier. But then again, maybe he was simply calculating. Because the towel made him look really, really hot— as did the fact that he was watching her as if he hadn't had nearly enough of her.

She paused at the mattress's edge, savoring the calendar shot he presented. Jack reached over and encircled her wrist, his fingers dark against her fair skin. He tugged and she tumbled to the bed, sinking into the comforter's soft down and bracing her hand against his solid chest. He released her wrist and feathered his fingers up her arm.

Another frisson of want shivered through her.

He plied his thumb along her shoulder. "You're a beautiful woman."

No, she wasn't. She was passably attractive. She caught herself before she argued the point. He wasn't trying to get her into bed—she was already here.

"Thank you. I'm sure I mentioned earlier that I find you devastatingly handsome." She traced the line where the white cotton towel met his flat belly. She watched in fascination as he stirred beneath the material.

"I don't want to devastate you, Eve."

There was a serious note in his voice but she blew off his comment, far too interested in the effect her marauding fingers were having on him. She'd transformed his towel into a tent.

"Jack, where are your condoms?"

The sudden consternation washing his aristocratic face verged on comical. "I'm out."

Not in her fantasy. "What do you mean you're out?"

"I keep one in my wallet and one in my shaving kit. Under normal circumstances I consider that prepared." Even "defensive" seemed sexy on this man.

"So, I'm an abnormal circumstance." Eve found herself inordinately pleased, although it shouldn't matter to her whether he carried two or twelve prophylactics with him when he traveled.

"Unique is a more apt description."

"You're right. I prefer unique to abnormal." Still, she wasn't about to let a matter of protection, or lack thereof, prematurely end her fling.

She picked up the bedside phone. One button connected her to room service.

"This is Steven. How may I help you?"

"Hi, Steven. I need some condoms delivered to Room four-fourteen, please."

"Certainly, ma'am." The smooth voice responded without missing a beat. The hotel wasn't joking when they boasted about their well-trained staff. "How many will you need and what is your preference?"

"What are the choices?"

"We have quite a selection—"

"If I take one of everything, how many is that?"

A slight pause. Steven counted under his breath. "Eight."

"Excellent. I'll take one of each."

"Somebody will be right up. Can I get anything else for you this evening?"

"No. That should take care of it. But I need those right away, Steven."

"Yes, ma'am."

She hung up.

"How many did you order?" Jack asked incredulously, winding a lock of her hair around his finger.

"Eight." She laughed at the mock horror on his face.

"Eight? You're going to give me a case of performance anxiety."

Her laughter melded into a sigh as he nuzzled the

tender skin beneath her chin. "I don't imagine you're anxious about much, especially your performance."

His lips teased the corner of hers. "There's always that first-time thing we discussed."

"I'd be glad to allay any of your anxiety. And there's no pressure to use them all. Just consider yourself restocked." He swallowed her last word in a teasing, playful kiss.

From the other room, a knock sounded on the suite door. Eve reluctantly pulled away. "That was prompt," she said, sliding toward the edge of the bed.

"I suppose they consider it somewhat urgent when you order in bulk." Jack levered himself off the bed with a grin. "Since you put in the order, the least I can do is get the door."

He ducked into the bathroom and came out shrugging into the hotel's white, monogrammed bathrobe. Eve halfheartedly listened as Jack answered the door, more focused on upcoming events than the conversation in the other room.

"Thank you. Let us know if we can get anything else for you, Mr. LaRoux."

Eve froze on the bed.

LaRoux. Jack LaRoux?

No, no, no.

Yes, yes, yes.

And she'd asked him to stand in for himself in this little fantasy. White-hot anger, laced liberally with humiliation, washed through her.

She'd kill him. Bare-handed.

She dismissed the notion as soon as it occurred. Too quick, too easy.

No. He'd beg for mercy before it was through. But it would be on her terms. Jack LaRoux was about to discover firsthand how Eve Carmichael earned the name Eve the Avenger.

5

JACK KNEW he was in for it. So much for how and when to divulge his true identity.

Regret tugged at him—that the situation had escalated to this point, that she'd had to find out this way, and, God help his selfish soul, that his trip with Eve Carmichael was over.

Jack thunked the silver-domed platter onto the coffee table. He had a snowball's chance in hell of running through the condom assortment with her now. He'd been so caught up in the past few hours, he hadn't thought through what would happen when they left his hotel room.

But he was thinking now. Fast. Three scenarios flashed through his head. Option one, she'd vilify him and then stomp out in a huff. Option two, she'd cry—God, he hoped she didn't cry. Or there was a remote chance, very remote, she'd laugh and they'd end up back in bed together.

Nix the last option. It was only wishful thinking brought about by all the great sex and the mess it had made of his brain. He *knew* this wasn't going to be pretty. At least he was wearing more than a towel. The silence in the next room, once intimate, now hung ominous and oppressive.

He squared his shoulders, as if to face a firing squad instead of a lover, and stepped into the bedroom.

Surprised, he stopped inside the doorway. Maybe she hadn't heard the room-service guy after all. She was still on the bed, propped on one side, intently tracing a pattern on the comforter with one finger *and* more importantly, she was still impressively naked.

He breathed a sigh of relief.

She looked up. "Where are they, Jack?" His name dripped off her tongue like venom and killed any hope he might have had that she hadn't heard. She appeared relaxed and composed, but her eyes radiated fury.

He stopped short of the bed, keeping his distance until this played out. "I left them in the other room. I didn't think we'd need them now."

"What's the matter? Are you only interested in women who don't know who you are? Or maybe you just have a thing for women who want you to pretend to be you. Which is it, Jack?" She smoothed her hair behind one ear, her sensuous movements and dulcet tone at odds with her rancorous words.

"Neither. It wasn't that way." He scrambled for footing on a slippery slope.

"Really?" Eve pursed her lips. "Then why don't you explain how it was for you." She sat up, propping herself on her elbows. "I'm all ears."

Not from where he stood.

"See," she continued. "I'm at something of a disadvantage because you knew how it was for me. But then that was part of it, wasn't it?"

He figured that now might not be the time to bring up how hot and sexy she was when she was angry.

"No—"

"No? Please. You can't expect me to believe that. Was I supposed to divulge my strategy for the account while basking in the afterglow?" She almost managed to mask the fury that underlaid her low, husky laugh. "Surely not. Or were you counting on a case of hysteria? Perhaps I'd back out of the competition, or at least be so humiliated, I'd be thrown off track?" She arched a brow. "How am I doing so far?"

"Not even close." *Pretty damn close.* No way in hell he was admitting it though.

Still, he'd never meant for her to feel humiliated by anything. How she took losing the vice presidency was up to her, but he hoped the experience didn't humiliate her. And that had nothing to do with the fact that they'd slept together. Convincing her was another matter.

"I didn't seek you out. You weren't even supposed to be here until Monday. I had no idea who you were when I first met you. I didn't even know what you looked liked." Although, he had to admit it, Eve the reality had turned out to be much better than the fantasy Eve he'd built in his head. "I thought you'd be a blonde. Well, a real blonde." He, who was usually very adept at coherent, even persuasive, conversation, stepped in it.

She narrowed her eyes. "When did you figure it out?"

His normal aplomb blown to hell, Jack instinctively,

and rather moronically, glanced at the dark curls between her thighs.

"Not the blonde part, Jack." The tone in her voice when she uttered his name made it sound like a four-letter word. And it was. "When did you figure out who I was?"

Not only was he not charming his way through this, but her nudity unnerved him. "When you gave me your first name, I checked the signature on the bar tab. As you'll recall, I'd already invited you to dinner." Love at first sight was hyperbole, but he'd admit to fascination at first sight. But he wasn't handing her that much power—not even to assuage her wounded pride. Because that's what this was all about.

"You didn't waste any time, though, did you?" she said.

He admitted a certain measure of guilt by omission, but she'd wanted him to pretend to be himself for God's sake. And it damn well took two to play. He wasn't looking for exoneration, but she could belly up to the bar of blame as well. "You didn't exactly run in the other direction, sweetheart," he countered.

"True enough." She raised her chin a notch and stiffened her spine, which made her bare breasts jiggle in the most distracting way. And he was a sick bastard, because seeing them jiggle, in turn, stiffened something other than his spine. She offered him a sweet, seductive smile he didn't trust. "Why don't you bring in those condoms, Jack?"

Lust, recrimination and wishful thinking had obviously combined to destroy his hearing. "Come again."

"Exactly."

"You're still..." Reluctant to make a fool of himself, he wouldn't utter the words.

"Interested? Turned-on? Of course." She slid off the bed and approached him. He swallowed hard. The seductive movement of her breasts, the sway of her hips, and the tangled cloud of hair around her shoulders bewitched him.

She stopped. The scent of recent sex clung to her and mingled with her perfume. Alluring. Arousing. Jack fisted his hands by his side to keep from reaching for her. Sex with an angry woman didn't strike him as the smartest plan.

She tugged one end of his belt and the robe fell open. She glanced down and her full lips curved into a smile. "Why, Jack, I see you're still interested as well."

There were some things a naked man couldn't hide. She slid her arms around his waist, her fingers molding into his back muscles, her nails scraping lightly against his skin.

His heart thundered, the throbbing desire she'd reawakened intensified.

"Eve, I don't think you really want to do this. Not this way." He cupped her shoulders to push her away. He hesitated, absorbing the heat and fine texture of her skin.

"Patronizing me right now would be a very bad idea." She smiled without humor. She leaned in and her nakedness whispered against his. "Before, it was just a fantasy...." She arched slightly, brushing her curls against his growing erection. "Let's see if Jack LaRoux is as good in reality."

As sexual penance, there were worse ways to pay for his sin of omission. She might've thought to hand him a massive case of performance anxiety, but, fortunately for both of them, Jack always performed well in tight spaces.

"I'LL BE RIGHT BACK." Jack turned and walked out of the bedroom. By rights, he should've looked fairly ridiculous with the white bathrobe billowing behind him. Instead he looked sexy.

Eve couldn't recall ever being this angry. Finding Perry and Delores in flagrante delicto desktop didn't begin to compare. And that in itself was disconcerting. As a rule, Eve didn't get angry.

A fair portion of her anger was self-directed because this loathsome man turned her on. She thought she'd been so smart, finding a suitable "fling" candidate, for using a surrogate lover to rid herself of Jack LaRoux's fantasy appeal. *Why don't I call you Jack?* Humiliation burned through her.

"Here they are. Just what you ordered." Jack brought the condoms in on a silver tray and placed it on the mattress's corner. His robe still hung open.

"Eve, I'm sorry things worked out this way. We can leave things the way they are."

No way in hell. She wanted her pound of flesh. She wanted him squirming.

"That seems like a waste of a good opportunity, not to mention an interesting condom assortment." And ultimately, this might prove to be a great opportunity for her.

She wound her arms around his neck, pulled his mouth down to hers and branded him.

His tongue answered her challenge and swept the tender regions of her mouth. Passion, lust and anger were a potent combination. It was a cruel twist of fate that this particular man stirred her to newfound depths, leaving her with a want fiercer than she'd ever known before.

Intensity, like a thin, taut string, connected them. It was no-holds-barred, gloves-off lovemaking. His mouth devoured hers. Her hands memorized his body, stroking, touching with bold intimacy. She fondled his hardened length. His moan reverberated in her mouth. She wrenched her mouth from his, rewarded by the sight of desire raging in his eyes.

"Do you like it when I touch you like that, Jack?" she asked in a low, husky tone.

"Yes. Can't you tell?" His voice was as strained as his sex.

She looked over the condom assortment. There was one chocolate. It wasn't Godiva, but it'd do.

She tore open the wrapper and unrolled the condom over the length of his erection, her fingers circling him at his base. He quivered in her hand.

She released him and pushed him back onto the bed, sending the condom-laden tray clattering to the floor. Eve crawled up after him. She explored his lean, muscular thighs, the flat plane of his belly, the expanse of flesh between his groin and hip with her hands and her mouth. The lightest strokes with her fingers followed by hot, sucking kisses and the occasional nip with her teeth.

Warm, masculine skin and the musky scent of his arousal surrounded her. The rapidly increasing harshness of his breathing told her she had him where she wanted him. Jack lay on his back, propped on his elbows, watching, waiting...

Her hair veiled his penis, teased against it. Her cheek occasionally brushed it as she feathered her lips against his skin. She plied her tongue along his inner thigh.

"Eve..."

She paused and looked up, her mouth hovered just above his straining erection. "Did you want something, Jack?"

"Yes."

"I'm not a psychic, Jack. Otherwise I would've known who you were from the beginning." She smiled, looking past his stiff member to his dark eyes.

"You don't need psychic powers when the matter at hand is staring you in the face."

She shook her head, deliberately brushing the weight of her hair across his sensitive tip. "But I don't like to assume anything." With a sigh, she bent forward to kiss his thigh, rubbing her cheek along his sheathed length. "And I always find that a nicely phrased request brings much more satisfying results. Don't you?" She looked up and exhaled, blowing gently against him.

"Please," he said, his face hard, his body rigid.

That was better, but it wasn't nearly enough. She wanted him pleading. And she hoped he did it soon, because all this teasing was leaving her in a bad way.

She was getting beaten at her own game. "Please? Please what?"

"Eve..."

"Jack, you really need to work on your communication skills." She traced her fingernail along the ridge of his scrotum.

"You're not going to be satisfied until you hear me beg are you?"

"I don't think either one of us will be actually satisfied, but we'd be well on our way."

"Would you please touch me?" he asked through gritted teeth.

Had Jack ever pleaded for anything? She doubted it. Even now he retained the arrogance she suspected he'd been born with and that boarding school had reinforced. The arrogance that set her teeth on edge. The arrogance she'd unwittingly pandered to when she'd asked him to pretend to be himself. Any discomfort she might've felt at exacting revenge was negated by that thought.

"But I've been touching you," she said, deliberately obtuse.

"Eve, touch my penis," he said.

She raised her eyebrows at his peremptory tone. They'd played the game by his rules before. If they were playing now, they were playing by her rules.

"Please."

She ran her finger along his rigid length. "Is that what you want?"

"Yes. No. More."

"It sounds as if you aren't sure what you really want, Jack."

Eve's college roommate had held the peculiar view that fellatio was a symbol of male domination. Ridiculous notion, because right now Eve knew beyond a doubt she wielded enormous power over Jack.

"Eve, would you please stop torturing me? I would beg harder, but I can't get any harder. I'm not even sure how much more conversation I'm capable of. If you're going to leave me this way, would you just go and stop tormenting me."

Actually she'd intended to arouse him and then leave him hanging. But now that didn't seem nearly as good an idea as it had been a few minutes ago. Primarily because she'd be left hanging, as well. In an attempt to arouse him, she'd also thoroughly turned herself on. She was throbbing and wet and eager to finish what she'd started. If she walked away now, she'd be *almost* as frustrated as she'd leave Jack.

She took him in her mouth and she felt the shudder that shook him. She didn't try to quell her own moan.

She might be the avenger, but she wasn't stupid.

EVE SLID to the edge of the bed. She had the same look in her eye she'd had when she'd finished her swim and her Scotch. She was finished with him and ready to move on. Unused to finding himself dismissed, Jack found himself curiously reluctant for Eve to leave.

"Why don't you stay?" Jack asked, trailing a finger down her naked back to a small strawberry-colored birthmark on her right hip.

Eve looked at him over her shoulder. "I don't knowingly do co-workers."

"Neither do I. Until now."

"I find that hard to believe, Jack. After all, you willingly slept with me and you knew damn well who I was."

He shouldn't care whether she believed him or not, but he did. He'd been attracted to a co-worker on more than one occasion. It was nearly impossible to spend the majority of your time at work and not develop attractions. But he'd never done anything about those attractions. Ever. Probably for the same reason Eve hadn't.

"I did know who you were. I hadn't had too much to drink. I wasn't coerced. I should've told you. It was bad judgment on my part." *Which led to some of the best sex of his life.* But not having lost all his brain cells in his last orgasm, he thought better of mentioning that. And that ought to have covered all his sins. He leaned forward and nuzzled the rounded, satin line of her shoulder. "But the damage is done."

"So you're saying why close the gate after the horse has already left the barn?" Eve leaned back, her body language belying her acerbic tone.

"Something like that."

She twisted around to face him, her movements sensual yet predatory. "I'm going to win, Jack."

"I know you're going to try."

Eve flicked her tongue against the lower lobe of his ear, eliciting an involuntary shiver from him. "Think what you want to. I'll be more than happy to have you on the team when I get that promotion."

He'd said much the same thing to Nev earlier. Somehow it wasn't nearly as palatable hearing it echoed back at him. He manipulated her to her back and leaned over her, supporting his weight on his forearms. "Will *you* work under *me* when I'm the boss?" he asked, choosing his words as deliberately as he'd chosen his position of domination.

"It's a non-issue, but no, I wouldn't. I have standards. I can only work for someone with integrity." Then, as if putting him down wasn't enough, she did that thing with her feet and had *him* on *his* back. "And you never told me whether I can count on you to be a team player when I'm in charge." From her position on top, she rimmed his ear with the warm, wet tip of her tongue, letting her breath fan against his neck, and her breasts tease his chest.

She was insulting the hell out of him and he was getting a hard-on. "What? I've got enough integrity to follow your orders but not to give them?"

She sat up, which removed her breasts from his chest, but firmly planted her bare bottom on his thigh. "Don't sound so offended. It's something like that."

He made a Herculean effort to focus on their discussion rather than her nakedness. "I don't think it has anything to do with integrity. But it has everything to do with losing."

"Well, you neatly avoided answering my question. Will you work for me, Jack?"

He had truly never considered the possibility that she might win. Probably because he was only thinking of himself. He knew instinctively he could never work under her and it had nothing to do with integrity. It was all a matter of power and position. It was also disconcerting to realize that Eve sincerely didn't like him. And even more disconcerting to realize that it actually *mattered* to him.

He rolled to his side, pulling her down with him, until she lay facing him. "No. I wouldn't work under you."

He cupped her breast in his left hand, thumbing her rosy nipple to a throbbing point. It was gratifying to see he could arouse her as easily as she aroused him.

Eve swept her hand between them and stroked his hardening length. "Well, I'm glad we got that issue cleared up."

And really, knowing she considered him lacking in integrity, he shouldn't sleep with her again. He should have enough pride to send her packing back to her room.

Eve rimmed the sensitive tip of his shaft with her fingers and pride took a back seat to the insatiable hunger she aroused in him. With a groan, he feasted on her lips, and gave himself over to the exquisite sensation of her touch.

Before long she broke his kiss, her hand still on his rigid length. "We need one of the condoms on the floor."

She might not like him, but she wanted him. And kicking Eve out of his bed at this point felt a good deal like cutting his nose off to spite his face.

"Are you getting it or should I?"

6

"WHERE ARE YOU GOING?" Jack asked, his arm tensing as she slid out from beneath it.

She'd thought he was out cold. Eve slid off the bed, the cool air prickling her skin with gooseflesh.

"My room." And she meant it this time.

He rolled onto his back, the sheets twisted about his lean hips, and crossed his arms beneath his head. Her heart rate quickened. These were desperate times when even his armpits struck her as sexy.

But she had to give credit when credit was due. Extraordinarily handsome, snake-in-the-grass Jack had debunked at least one myth this evening. *This* gorgeous man had put a lot of effort into her satisfaction. More than anyone before him had ever done, and with gratifying result.

"What's the rush?" he asked. His glance slid over her nakedness, his eyes full of slumberous heat.

"I wouldn't exactly call it a rush. I've been here for more than six hours." Eve forced herself to look away before she gave in and dove back under those same sheets with him.

Ideas for the new campaign had already started streaming through her head and she really needed to get back to her room to jot them down before she forgot. Besides, there was an intimacy in cocooning beneath the sheets with Jack and drifting off into unguarded sleep that struck her as a bad move.

She scooped her bra and pumps from beneath the edge of the bed and walked into the adjoining room.

"Anyway, I'm inspired to work," she said, plucking her panties and her purse from the sofa cushion. She heard his measured tread and stuffed her underwear into her purse.

Jack joined her, belting the robe around him and looking sexier than he had a right to. She'd been on target with her first estimation. He was lethal and the women of the world deserved a warning label.

"Want to talk about it? We could brainstorm," he offered, a devilish smile curling his lip, lighting his eyes. "I'm pretty good at it."

No doubt. He'd been *very* good at everything so far—except in offering the truth. Eve laughed and forced herself not to clutch her purse in front of her like a small, black shield. Jack the Ripper was sexy *and* incorrigible.

"You were good, Jack, but not that good. I had an orgasm, not a lobotomy." Nice delivery. Droll with a hint of exasperated amusement. A nice cover for the effect he had on her.

He shrugged and lifted one brow, humor glinting in his slate-gray eyes. "It was worth a try."

"It's always worth a try, isn't it?"

A delicious heat spread through her. She wanted him. There was no doubt about it, Jack did it for her. But did he consider her a total twit, thinking that a good toss in the sack and a measure of insouciant charm would bail him out of his earlier scam?

She slid her feet into her pumps and walked over to her dress, puddled by the door. Eve stepped into the dress and bent down to pull it up.

"If you're serious about leaving, you might not want to bend over naked like that any more. Now, *that's* inspiring." A husky note threaded his voice.

She'd had more sex in the past six hours than the past six months. Well, technically the last year, but then she lost the parallel construction of the comparison. Anyhow, she'd used parts tonight that she hadn't used in quite a while and she was very aware of them. But one long, slow look, a hoarse note from Jack, and her entire body became one big erogenous zone.

She tugged the zipper up as far as it would go, loath to go through the undignified contortions necessary to wrestle it all the way. As if it mattered anyway. How many people was she likely to bump into in the hallway at this hour?

"There. Is that better?" she asked.

"Almost." He moved to stand beside her, his scent teasing her. "Let me get that for you."

She wasn't sure if she could bear his hands on her right now, but she'd be damned if she'd let him know just how powerfully he affected her. She turned her back to him.

He clasped her dress in one hand. Slowly, deliberately he slid the tab up with the other, his knuckles playing against her bare skin, his breath warm against her neck and back, turning the simple act of dressing into a subtle form of foreplay.

"That should be better—" he cupped her shoulders in his hands and fire raced along her nerve endings "—but it isn't. I know you're not wearing anything under it."

"It's one way to avoid panty lines." The words started out a clever quip, but the heat building inside her lent her voice a smoky quality.

He slid his hands over her hips. "Definitely no panty lines," he murmured behind her ear. Her pulse raced in a frantic dance. "You're inspired to work, but you've inspired me in other ways."

Eve turned to face Jack. Leaving didn't seem quite as urgent as it had thirty seconds before. "And what's so inspiring about a lack of underwear?"

He stepped toward her and despite their banter, she retreated, the wall a solid force behind her.

"Surely that's a rhetorical question." He skimmed his hand from her hip, across her belly and breast, and eased her dress strap over her shoulder with one finger. He trailed his fingers down her chest and reached beneath the neckline and freed her breast. "Because it's so easy to do this." He thumbed the engorged tip and she was on fire.

She ran her tongue along her suddenly-gone-dry lips.

"Or this." He dipped his dark head to her breast and lapped the sensitive peak.

She buried her fingers into his hair and pulled him closer. Obligingly, wordlessly, his mouth captured her nipple and sucked. She arched against him, thrusting her nipple more firmly in his mouth, glad of the support of the wall behind her.

How could she dislike him so intensely yet love the things he did to her body? "Harder," she instructed with a rasp.

He did. She gasped and then moaned at the sensation of his mouth tugging at her nipple. Jack reached beneath her dress with his other hand and grasped her bare buttock, squeezing her bottom. Instinctively she braced her legs further apart, opening herself to him.

Releasing her, yet relentlessly suckling her, Jack slid his fingers along her swollen cleft. She bucked against his hand, desperate for something more than that teasing touch. His moan reverberated against her breast.

He slipped his hands beneath the edge of her dress and lifted it to her waist. He knelt before her and Eve reminded herself to breathe.

She leaned back and shifted her legs apart. Anticipation had her holding on to the wallpapered foyer for support. Then Jack wrapped his long fingers around her thighs and bent his head. His warm breath whispered on her skin. Seeing his dark head against her pale thighs turned her on even more. He parted her with his thumbs, her sensitive flesh quivering at the close contact. *Oh, yes.* And then he dipped his head a fraction and intimately kissed her.

Oh. My. His lips molded to her, plied her tender fold, drank from her.

"Hmm." The vibration from his mouth hummed

through her. "You taste so sweet, Eve," he said, his voice muffled, his lips tickling against her.

By way of an answer, Eve leaned against the wall and thrust against him. His mouth and tongue teased and tormented her beyond coherent words, warm, wet, relentless, coaxing, demanding until she shattered into tiny fragments like a kaleidoscope pattern—fragmented but complete, a thing of beauty that, with the tiniest movement, would shift and take on another form.

She blinked, opening her eyes. When had she closed them? She struggled to tug the remnants of her control back into place.

Jack stood, releasing the hem of her dress. And oddly enough, he looked as satisfied as she felt. Well, almost. Somehow a polite thank-you seemed inane but she had to say something. "Wow."

Please, tell her she hadn't just said "wow." Maybe she *had* experienced a lobotomy right along with that last orgasm.

"I told you I found your lack of underwear inspiring," Jack said, looking altogether too pleased with himself and the situation.

Eve pressed a hard, hot kiss on his mouth, tasting her musky scent on his lips.

"Then I'll have to seriously consider going commando for our Monday-morning meeting," she said, stepping out of his room, leaving him something to think about.

JACK FINISHED the last note on his laptop and looked up, surprised at the burgeoning dawn seeping along the horizon's edge in shades of pink. He'd started out only making a few notes, but before long his adrenaline was pumping and the ideas were flowing. He stretched and rolled his shoulders. By rights, he should be exhausted. Instead, he was exhilarated. He felt more alive than he had in a very long time. Eve had blown into his life like a gust of fresh air. Nev had been right. After releasing a few endorphins, he'd done his best work this morning, roughing out some awesome creative ideas.

Too bad he couldn't tell Nev that Eve Carmichael was his inspiration. And he *couldn't* tell Nev. Jack trusted Nev with a lot. His career. His back. But what if Nev slipped up and said something to the wrong person? Eve would be ruined. And while Jack meant to have that promotion, he found his ruthlessness tempered by a reluctance to decimate Eve in the process. With a start, he realized that alien feeling was compassion. Twenty-four hours ago he wouldn't have cared about decimating her. He'd always believed in survival of the fittest in business and it had worked so far. He shrugged off the notion he might be going soft. He didn't need to ruin Eve's reputation to win this account.

No woman had ever stuck so firmly in his mind afterward. Jack excelled at compartmentalizing his thoughts, emotions, people. A neat little survival trick he'd learned at an early age growing up in the LaRoux household. However, Eve had stubbornly planted herself in his psyche and refused to budge.

Just thinking about her, tasting her against his lips, catching the faint whiff of her scent that lingered against his skin awoke a latent hunger in him.

He had a couple of choices. He knew Eve's room number. He could pull on some clothes and stop by Room 325—her name and room number in her elegant scrawl were seared in his brain—and see if he could talk her into a little daybreak sex. Or, he could take matters into his own hands, which he hadn't had to resort to since his early days of puberty. His third option was to pull on a pair of running shorts, a T-shirt, and put in a few miles.

Jack reached for his shorts. There was nothing that a good hard run couldn't cure—including infatuation.

EVE PRESSED her fingertips against the cool glass of the window. Low, dark clouds rolled in from the east, chasing away the pink-hued promise of a sunny day. A shopkeeper on the corner opposite the hotel swept the sidewalk fronting his store. Eve smiled to herself. He reminded her of Mr. Abruzzi at home. A woman with big, frizzy red hair walked by, bearing a striking resemblance to her leashed Pomeranian. A lone runner loped into view.

Jack. She'd known him less than twenty-four hours and already she recognized the arrogant tilt to his dark head, the span of his shoulders, the length of muscular legs. A double Pavlovian response rippled through her. Antipathy and arousal. Her simultaneous dislike and desire confounded her.

He raised his head and looked right at her. A slow

smile curled his mouth. Unbidden, an intense craving for the feel of that sensual mouth—on her mouth, her sex, her breasts—ravaged her.

She stepped away from the window, hoping that might dispel the ache for him. She couldn't just stand around aroused like some lust-struck ninny. Instead she saved her notes once again before she turned her computer off. She shoved her crude sketches—she was no artist, for sure—of streamlined, lighter and more stylish farm equipment she'd market to the untapped market of women who ran their own operations, into her attaché. She didn't trust Jack any further than she could throw him. And he'd be here soon. She knew it.

When she'd finally made it back to her room this morning, she'd showered. But what she needed before she found herself face-to-face, or flesh-to-flesh as was more likely the case, with Jack again was a good, hot soak. She padded across the carpet to the tiled bathroom and turned on the hot water, adding just a trickle of cold to temper the heat. She dumped in a generous measure of bath gelée compliments of the hotel.

A knock resounded through her room. Jack? She left the bathroom and peered through the peephole. Yes, Jack. She'd have bet money that Mr. Gorgeous would've showered and shaved before he showed up. For an instant, she considered turning him away, but dismissed the thought as soon as it occurred. No way would she let him think she was running away from him. She'd meet him head-on at every encounter. And he still looked yumm-o, even in sweaty running clothes.

Eve flipped the safety lock and opened the door.

"Your paper." Jack held out the newspaper that had been outside her door, compliments of the hotel.

"How did you know what room I was in?" she asked, moving aside to let him in.

"You signed your room number as well as your name on the bar tab last night." His look slid over her, the heat in his eyes scorching her. She forced herself not to shift her weight from foot to foot like some nervous schoolgirl. "I thought that was you in the window," he said grinning.

"So, that was you running?" Let him think she wasn't sure. It was a far better option than cluing him into the fact that she'd spotted him dead on at a distance.

"You look good in red." His lingering look told her just how good.

Her heart pounded and moisture gathered between her thighs. She was like a bitch in heat every time he was around.

"I have a weakness for nice lingerie. And who wouldn't look decent in red silk?" Her wardrobe might be all business, but her undergarments were purely for her own pleasure. And apparently now Jack's.

He shook his head, a wolfish expression on his lean, stubbled face. "More along the lines of enticingly indecent." Her nipples tightened beneath the material and his smile was a wicked acknowledgment. "Not decent at all. Is this a bad time?" he asked, inclining his head toward the running water.

Her body reacted to the promise of pleasure to come. "It depends on what you're here for. I was about to take a bath."

"I could use a bath." Sweat stained his T-shirt. Running shorts showed off his muscled thighs and calves. For such a lean guy, he boasted nicely muscled legs. Heat spiraled through her. Who was she kidding? He boasted a nice *everything*.

"Keep your friends close and your enemies closer?" she suggested.

"I don't want to be your enemy, Eve." He traced his finger along the line where the red silk plunged to mid-navel.

His touch whispered against her skin, trailing heat against her, through her. "What do you want to be, Jack?"

"I liked being your fantasy."

"You must like taking risks. Most men wouldn't want to bring that up again."

"But you have to be willing to take a few risks if you want big payoffs."

"What do you consider a big payoff?"

"Being back in bed with you." Oh, my. Sweet phrases were overrated. There was something very erotic when a sexy man stated in blunt, unadorned terms that he wanted you. "And I don't want us to be enemies."

"Come on, Jack. I would've sworn there wasn't a naive bone in your body. You and I both know that what one wants isn't necessarily what one gets. We can have a weekend of great sex, but we're still two dogs fighting over the same bone. Regardless of how good we are in bed, nothing changes that." She walked around him and into the bathroom, turning off the tap. Fragrant steam rose from the water. "Now, I'm taking a bath. You can leave...." They both knew where they were going to wind up, knew how they affected the other one. But that didn't mean she had to make it easy for him. He'd gotten off way too easy yesterday. "Or you can come in and watch," she said over her shoulder as she moved to the vanity.

"Keep your enemies close?" he asked, approaching behind her.

She pulled her hair up off her neck and shoulders and clipped it into a loose twist. "The closer the better," she said to his reflection in the mirror.

He took her shoulders in his hands. His breath was warm against her neck, his hands dark against her fairness. "How close do I need to be to satisfy you on that point?" He wrapped his arms around her and cupped her silk-covered breasts in his hands. His bristled chin scraped deliciously against her neck and shoulder. His erection nudged at her buttocks. Both of them watched in the mirror. There was nothing cool or remote about him now. He was hard and hot, and even sweat smelled good on him.

"I think even a little closer yet." She wriggled against his erection.

His eyes held hers in the mirror. "I don't think I'm going to be content to just watch...."

No, it wasn't going to be nearly enough. "Jack, do you have any condoms with you?"

He swore softly. "I don't usually need them when I'm out running. Don't you have some?"

"I don't usually need them. Period."

"Then I can only say that very few men have seen you in that particular nightgown. Or better yet, out of it." He slid her straps down her arms, exposing her pink-tipped breasts. His eyes darkened.

He turned away from her. "I'll be right back."

He was leaving? Now? He laughed softly at her quizzical look.

"*I'm* making the room-service call this time."

7

RAIN SLANTED horizontally against the windows where Eve had left the curtains open, lending the room a lazy, rainy-day intimacy.

"I'm starving," Jack said, rolling over. His bare hip pressed against her thigh. "I don't think either of us ate any real food last night."

Her last meal was a distant memory. When she was engrossed in work, she forgot all about eating. And up until a few minutes ago, she'd been extremely distracted by Jack. Now she was hungry enough to gnaw on the bedpost. "I'm ravenous."

"Do you want to go somewhere..." He trailed off in obvious reluctance.

The perversity of spending the day naked, having really great sex with the man she'd soon face off against appealed to her. Perhaps she was sick. Maybe she was stupid. It could be a bad combination of both, but right now it simply felt good and she was rolling with it. She was going to wring every ounce of opportunity out of this weekend fling. Eve shook her head. "Room service."

"Excellent idea. So far, room service has been very, very good to us." Jack's teeth gleamed white against his day-old beard. She was oddly glad that Jack hadn't shaved before his run—somehow that would've seemed too fussy, too affected, too vain. Good thing she was flat on her back when he smiled like that, because, quite frankly, she doubted her knees' ability to support her.

Eve's mother would call Jack a smooth talker. And he was. But Eve had his number. And she couldn't make a bad man decision if her eyes were wide-open, could she? As far as all her previous bad men choices went, at least Jack was an exceptional lover, possessed a sense of humor, and didn't seem nearly as narcissistic as some of the other men she'd dated. And none of them had been spine-tingling sexy like Jack. Trustworthiness was only an issue if a gal was looking for a commitment. And she most definitely wasn't.

"What do you want?" she asked.

With a wicked smile, he lifted one of her breasts in his hand, intimately toying with her nipple, as if he couldn't keep his hands to himself. His touch vibrated through her.

She wasn't quite sure whether he was better for her libido or her ego. Both were pretty happy with his attention. She sat up. "I meant what do you want from room service? There's a menu around here somewhere," she said.

Jack pulled her back down. "I don't need a menu." He drew a lazy circle around her breast with his index finger. "If room service can deliver condoms twice, they can surely bring us whatever we want to eat. What's your favorite breakfast food?"

Eve didn't hesitate. "Fruit and chocolate. Nothing is better than chocolate."

"Nothing?" Jack asked, with a smirk and a raised brow.

"Sorry. You're good but chocolate is chocolate."

"Hmm. That sounds like a challenge."

Eve shrugged. "It's not a challenge. Merely a fact."

"I'll have to see if I can't find something you like even better than chocolate."

"I doubt that's possible...but I'd love to see you try."

"I'll work on that after breakfast. Orange juice and champagne?"

She wouldn't allow herself to be sucked up into the romantic aspects of champagne in bed on a rainy day. With Jack. Still, she had to drink something.... "So far, so good."

"Eggs Benedict?"

"Is that a signature dish for you?" she asked, unable to refrain from alluding to Benedict Arnold, who'd earned a spot in history with his traitorous deception.

Jack had the grace to look slightly abashed. "I thought I paid that debt."

"I'll aim for civility."

"Maybe food will improve your humor."

"I *am* hungry, so it's in your best interest to keep me happy."

"I'm all about my best interests," he said.

"Tell me something I didn't already know."

"Are you always so acid-tongued?"

"Only with special people."

"Let me order before you wound me past recovery." Eve admired the play of muscles in his shoulders and down his back as he placed their breakfast order. She didn't trust him, not even for a minute, and she was sure he didn't trust her, but she definitely didn't find his company boring. Jack hung up the phone and turned to her.

"They weren't sure how long it would take. And you'll have to answer the door because I don't have any dry clothes," Jack said with a laugh, seemingly not too concerned.

"Give me your room key and I'll run down and pick up a couple of things for you," she offered with a smirk.

"That's generous, Eve. Really it is, considering you'd be alone in my room with my notes and my laptop. But my running clothes will dry sooner or later."

"That'll teach you to climb into a tub fully clothed. And I think you just implied you don't trust me."

"Was I that subtle? Sweetling, I *don't* trust you at all."

"Why, Jack, you've hurt my feelings." Not. It's exactly what she'd thought less than a minute ago, but she needed to clear up a point for him. "Seriously, I'd never steal your ideas to win."

Jack wore scepticism as well as he wore everything else. Or, considering his impressively naked state, as well as he didn't wear anything at all. "Then I overestimated how much you want this."

Ha. He had no clue how much she wanted this. She'd consider selling her Granny Carmichael if that's what it took to get this promotion. Mercifully, it shouldn't be necessary. Although it wasn't as compromising as it sounded since she really didn't like her grandmother. Granny Carmichael was mean as hell and had never particularly liked Eve.

"Oh, I want it. It's not about that. I simply don't need to steal to win. I've got a strong team backing me and I'm good enough on my own." And she was going to score big on innovation with her segue into the women's market.

Jack nodded. "I've seen your work. You're very good."

"Worried?"

"No."

His slightly patronizing smile indicated she might be good but he was better. Fine. Let him underestimate her. "How did you get involved in advertising?"

Other than a quirk of his brow, he rolled with her subject change. "I liked the balance between creative and business. What about you?"

"I was hooked from my first college course. Pulling together an ad campaign's a puzzle where all the pieces need to fit." It wasn't just a career choice, it was a passion.

"Nice analogy. And where does your personal life fit in the puzzle that's Eve?"

She shook her head. "I'm no puzzle at all. I spend the majority of my time at work because I love what I do. I'm good at it and that makes me feel good about myself." And because she was driven to always push harder. Whatever she achieved never seemed enough.

"No boyfriend waiting on you in New York?"

The odds struck her as zero to none that the gossip line at Hendley and Wells hadn't filled him in on the Perry episode, but she sure as hell wasn't going to bring up that particular morsel of embarrassment— especially while she was lounging in bed with him. "No one's waiting on me anywhere. Work doesn't leave a lot of time for relationships and quite frankly, it's usually not worth the effort required."

From what she'd seen, relationships with men weren't about giving—they were about giving up. Career. Freedom. Yourself.

"That doesn't sound like the woman who defended true love last night."

Interesting that he wanted to examine her and her theories of love under a microscope. Eve felt a bit like a case study rather than a human being. He commented on a topic and then sat back and watched for a reaction. What about him? "Why are you concerned with something you don't believe in? What'd you call love—a shadow puppet? What makes you such a cynic, Jack?" Eve held up a hand. "And don't tell me life. That's too easy."

"I'd say you were running a tight second in the cynical arena."

"I'm not cynical, merely cautious. And once again you neatly sidestepped my question."

"Oh, yes, the burning issue of my cynicism. How about a *lifetime* of observation?"

That nailed it. It was as if he was observing her rather than interacting with her. And his cynicism would've been easier to take if he'd displayed a hard, bitter edge. Instead, Eve found his almost weary acceptance wrenching.

"I hope one day you find someone who proves you wrong and restores your faith," Eve said.

"My faith in what?"

"Mankind. Love."

"Are you volunteering?" he asked.

"Perish the thought." Eve laughed, equally horrified and amused. She wasn't looking for a relationship, especially with a man like him.

Jack flashed a grin, but something indefinable lurked behind the amusement glinting in his eyes. "Should I surmise from that bark of laughter and vehement denial that you find me unlovable?"

"It's nothing personal. I'm sure the right woman is out there just waiting for you to notice her."

"Why not you, Eve?" A taunting note edged his tone.

Thank you, but no thank you. Not in this lifetime, at least while she was still in charge of all of her faculties. Jack LaRoux as a love interest was a disaster waiting to happen.

She wasn't a cynic of Jack's caliber, but neither was she naive. If Jack truly thought her interested, he'd run like hell in the opposite direction. "I'm not very good with needy people."

"Needy?" His eyebrows slanted further up, lending his handsome face a decidedly wicked aspect. Despite his smile, his voice had a hard edge.

Okay, maybe she'd overstepped her bounds with

that comment. But the boundaries between them had been skewed from the moment she met him. And now that she'd said it, she'd stand her ground. "Anyone with your level of cynicism strikes me as needy."

"And you're not up to the task?"

She was no fool. Jack wasn't particularly interested in her. Her lack of interest in the position was what had piqued his curiosity. She felt sure on a bad day, women would line up to fill the position of pumping life back into Jack's cynical heart.

"Nope. Not me. My younger brother Bryan handles all the needy people. He's a Methodist minister." Bryan had cornered the market on compassion. Eve wasn't nearly as tolerant.

"I don't think your brother Bryan's my type," Jack drawled.

"I wouldn't think so. But then again, I'm one-hundred-percent sure I'm not your type, either." She wasn't fishing. She knew Jack's type. She'd pegged him from the beginning. Sleek, high-maintenance women. She still wasn't sure why she'd caught his eye, but she knew for sure she wasn't the norm.

"Maybe that's the problem. Maybe I've just been looking for the wrong type of woman to cure my neediness."

"Probably."

"Aren't you compelled to save me from myself?"

She managed to bite back a *Hell, no.* "Hardly." His sarcasm didn't surprise her. Being pegged needy wasn't particularly flattering, especially for someone like Jack, who seemingly had it all and needed nothing. It was time to lighten this up. "Are you professing undying devotion?"

"Would it do me any good if I was?"

"No. But don't despair. There are plenty of women out there who'd see you as better than a Weight Watcher's extra point."

Jack looked startled and then relaxed onto the pillow, chuckling. "Eve Carmichael, you are truly one of a kind. You don't pull any punches, do you? I'm damn glad I'm here with you on this rainy morning in Chicago. Even if you do find me unlovable and needy."

"Don't put words in my mouth. There's lovable—" she slid her lips across his, her skin tingling with the rasp of his beard "—and then there's lovable. And there's needy—" she lightly scraped her nails across his flat stomach "—and there's needy."

"And what do you need, Eve?"

They wouldn't go there. "Breakfast would be a good start. Room service is much faster with condoms than food. Until it arrives, you're filling in nicely."

Jack captured her marauding fingers in his and trapped her wrist at her side. "I really want to know. What do you need?" He pierced her with his gray gaze.

"This promotion. That's what I need, Jack."

"I'm thinking more along the lines that you need someone to protect you from your naivety if you believe I need to be saved from myself."

"You're wrong on both counts. I'm not naive and I don't need a protector. I'm no damsel in distress." God, it was the same mentality her family carried.

Why couldn't they see her as the self-sufficient, assured, successful woman she was?

"Often the people who need protecting the most realize it the least."

She'd play his own game with him. "Are you volunteering to be my white knight, Jack?"

A knock sounded on the door. Food. Jack released her wrists, his fingers lingering on her pulse.

"No." His smile wasn't particularly nice, but then he wasn't a particularly nice man. "Maybe I'm the one you need protection from, Eve."

JACK ADDED a touch more sauce and polished off the last of his eggs Benedict, trying to shake the annoyance still clinging to him. Quite frankly, he wasn't sure if he was more annoyed with Eve deeming him needy or himself because her comment mattered to him. Eve's opinion should carry no more weight than a stranger's on the street. Except, somewhere between the initial moment of attraction and now, he'd come to respect her. He liked her, even. It wasn't that he disliked people as a rule. But generally, he was ambivalent. He pushed aside the empty plate and sat back.

"They're wonderful. Try it," Eve said, offering a chocolate-dipped strawberry. She'd passed on the eggs and gone straight for the chocolate and fruit.

Jack bit into it. "Delicious."

"I told you, chocolate makes everything better," Eve said, obviously enjoying hers.

She had actually said nothing was better than chocolate, but she was so obviously enjoying it, why argue the point? She sat on the small sofa, one leg tucked beneath her, the red silk gown clinging and plunging in all the appropriate places. Having sated one appetite, another made itself known. You would think he could make it through breakfast without wanting her again. That, however, was not the case. And while Jack didn't necessarily *take* what he wanted, he was used to *getting* what he wanted.

"So, chocolate makes everything better? Let's see." Jack leaned over and licked a small smear of chocolate at the corner of her generous mouth. "I think you may be on to something."

"Well, if we're testing the theory..." She gathered chocolate on the tip of her finger with one swipe along the fruit tray, circled his nipple with her finger, then dragged her finger across his chest to his other nipple. Her touch alone ricocheted through him. His shudder was wholly involuntary. He was glad he'd opted to knot a towel around his waist instead of the hotel robe. Actually, following that train of thought, it would've been good to be totally naked if she was looking for taste test sites.

Eve smiled, much like a cat cornering a canary, dipped her head and licked the chocolate from the path she'd just created. Jack closed his eyes and absorbed the sensation of her warm, wet tongue delicately lapping at his skin.

"Now that was tasty," she said.

Jack opened his eyes. The cooler air kissed his skin where her warm tongue had just traveled, lending its own sensation. Tasty? Try erotic.

He'd started this, and she seemed more than willing to continue.

"I think I should try it again." He plucked a red berry with its dark coating from the plate and bit off the end of the fruit. It was tart and sweet all at the same time, but not nearly as good as it was served up on Eve. He trailed the fruit and chocolate down the column of her throat, along her collarbone to the top of her breast left bare by the red silk gown.

Eve, her head thrown back, murmured something that sounded close to "Oh, my," and ended on a sigh.

Jack had never been into food games in the bedroom. He'd dated a girl in college—was it Mandy, or perhaps it had been Samantha—who had brought along a jar of honey one night. He'd indulged her, but it hadn't been like this, where just the sight of the chocolate and strawberry against Eve's pale skin left him aching.

But not aching to the point of no control. No, Eve was the one he wanted out of control. What did she know about him? Nothing that he didn't want her to. He'd spent a lifetime making sure he didn't need anyone or anything. Being shipped off to boarding school at a young age had taught him well. How dare she call him needy and then tell him in the next breath he'd be lucky to find a woman willing to take him on. The only thing he needed now was to taste her skin, feel her tremble, hear her scream his name as they both found intense pleasure in each other. It was purely physical. You walked away at the end of it. Nice and uncomplicated.

Jack sampled his way down the luscious trail, further aroused by the pounding of her heart beneath his cheek, the delicate quiver that raced across her skin as his lips nuzzled chocolate and strawberry from the soft rise of her breast. "Now that is a tasty morsel."

Eve's laugh was breathless. "You are decadent."

Unlovable. Needy. Now decadent. Her opinion of him just got better and better. He'd never been unsure of himself with a woman before. Or so damn insecure. This wasn't even close to what he had in mind when he thought of the "first" experiences awaiting him with Eve. "I prefer to think of myself as a connoisseur of the finer things. Are you complaining?"

Her aquamarine eyes shimmered with heat. "Only if you're stopping."

"You just have to say the word and I will."

"I'm hoping you won't." Her husky voice set his pulse pounding. He was there. The champagne bottle caught his eye.

"I've worked up quite a thirst. Champagne would go nicely with that, don't you think?" he said.

"I think it would be very...refreshing."

Jack pulled the bottle from the ice bucket. He rolled the cold glass across her silk-clad breasts. Eve's sharp indrawn breath hissed in the room's quiet. "Too cold?" He held the bottle away from her body.

"It's just right." She arched her back, thrusting her chest against the hard surface.

Jack's mouth went dry and heat roared through him. His hand shook as he poured a small amount of champagne over her pebbled tip.

"Oh...yes. Ahh." He bent forward and took her swollen, champagne-soaked, silk-covered nipple into his warm mouth. She was so sweet. He sucked the sparkling beverage off the cloth, drawing her harder and firmer into his mouth. The taste of her and her whimpers fed his pleasure. Jack released her.

His heart pounded as if he'd run a marathon. "Much better than drinking from a glass."

She twisted, offering her other breast. "They come in a pair. Try this one and see which one you prefer."

They were early on in the game and already he was rock hard. He chuckled. "And you thought *I* was decadent?"

"You are. It must be catching. And I know just the cure." She took the bottle from him and rubbed the thick rim along her other nipple. The elongated point beckoned to him. She breathed more harshly as she poured a small stream of pale liquid over her breast. "Served for your pleasure." He swooped, capturing her turgid point in his mouth, once against suckling her. "And mine. Definitely my pleasure..." She trailed off.

The last word ended in a moan as he flicked the tip with his tongue. He raised his head. "I think you liked that. Almost as much as I did."

"Mmm." Eve plucked another strawberry from the plate. Her eyes never left his as she crushed the berry and smeared strawberry and chocolate on her breast. She delved beneath the edge of her gown, coating her nipple. She repeated it on the other side until they were covered with the sticky mixture. She brought her hand to her mouth, sucking her fingers clean, one by one. Every time she took a digit into her mouth, his sex quivered as if she were taking him deep into her warm, wet mouth. When the last finger was clean, she offered herself to him. *"Bon appétit."*

Again he pulled the champagne from the bucket. "Fruit, chocolate and champagne go best when they're all tasted at once," he said, just before he poured more champagne over her. Instead of returning the bottle to the bucket, he settled it between her thighs. She spread her legs further apart and he cradled it there more firmly, then bent forward, trapping the bottle between them. She shifted, rubbing herself against the bottle.

He dealt in sensual imagery on a daily basis. Bottom line in advertising, sex sold. The phallic imagery of the champagne bottle nestled between her thighs, the dark, soaked silk covering her full breasts, the arousal reflected in her eyes, the scent of champagne, chocolate, fruit and sex was beyond intoxicating. And perhaps most arousing of all was her hedonistic pleasure in the experience. She'd smeared that fruit on herself not to turn him on but because she liked the way it felt.

"Eve..."

"Do you like what you see, Jack?"

"You are so hot."

"You haven't lost your appetite, have you?"

She awakened appetites he never knew he had. He'd never been so hungry for someone in his life. "I'm ravenous."

He leaned over her and lost himself in the taste of

champagne, chocolate, strawberry mingled against his tongue with the taste of Eve. The harder he suckled the more intense the flavor and the deeper and throatier her cries.

Caught up in the erotic game playing out between them, Jack discovered a new facet of himself. One not driven by calculating the odds. A desire to arouse and satisfy beyond anything he'd ever known before.

They were out of strawberries. He'd eaten the eggs. But the small pitcher of hollandaise sauce continued to warm over the burner. Thick rich sauce trailed over satin skin and red silk...

"All that sugar has given me a taste for something salty. And we still have perfectly good hollandaise sauce left." He dipped his finger into the sauce and held it out to her. She took his finger into her mouth and swirled her tongue around it. Oh, yes. She released him, her tongue licking her lips as if seeking any residual.

"Mmm. Very nice. Just the right amount of lemon— subtle. I don't like it when it's too obvious. I can see how that would whet your appetite."

He was so whetted he throbbed. "Stand up, Eve, and turn around."

She stood and presented her back to him. Her gown's back plunged even farther than the front, leaving her creamy skin exposed along the length of her spine, past her waist, to the beginning curve of her buttocks with their sexy, matching dimples. "You have outstanding taste in lingerie."

She glanced over her shoulder, her hair tangled, her

eyes alight with a provocative mix of humor and arousal. She slid her hands over her hips, as if she relished the texture of the silk beneath her fingertips and against her skin. She was possibly the most naturally sensual, unselfconscious woman he'd ever met. "*I* like it."

She pleased herself and didn't particularly care whether it met with his approval at all. And that in itself was a turn-on. He wasn't pressed to respond in a certain way.

"Your gown is ruined...or it's about to be."

"I have more and I can always buy another. But we're about to make a raging mess for room service to clean up."

Jack unknotted the towel at his waist and dropped it at her feet. One step back and she stood on the thick cotton.

"Better?" he asked.

"Much." Her hot glance flicked over him, lingering on his jutting, throbbing sex. "And it definitely improves the view. I should've been concerned sooner."

He grinned at her appreciation of his nakedness. Eve intrigued him. Confounded him. Aroused him. Immeasurably.

"Jack..."

"Yes?"

"What are you waiting for?"

Her subtle impatience tightened the knot of sexual tension inside him.

He picked up the handled bowl with its spout and tipped it over her back at the indent of her waist.

Sauce disappeared beneath the edge of her gown, between the mounds of her buttocks. Visually it was very...stimulating.

"Oh, Jack. It feels good. Hot and thick." She leaned forward, directing the flow.

"Does that mean you want more?" His voice was as hot and thick as her description. Her sexy talk, the sight of her, and the sweet musk of her arousal perfuming the air slammed him, destroying all his objectivity in one fell swoop. Engaged him. He became a participant rather than an observer.

"Yes."

Jack tilted the bowl again, his hand shaking so damn much he was surprised he didn't drop it.

"Brace your knee on the love seat and lean over."

She bent over and he raised the hem of her gown, exposing her buttocks with their coating of rich sauce. He squeezed her plump cheeks together, his fingers sliding in the creamy sauce.

Kneeling, he licked first one buttock, then the other clean. She shuddered and arched her back, thrusting toward him. The butter from the sauce left her slippery. "Oh, Eve. That is tasty. Much better on you than on the eggs."

He traced his tongue along her skin sucking at the tempting flesh that was the underside of her cheek, where it met her thigh, to the back of her knee. She trembled. Or perhaps he was the one quivering.

"You're right, Eve. I am needy. I need to be inside you like never before."

"Then we need the same thing, Jack." She looked

over her shoulder, her breathing harsh, her eyes hot. "But this time, we can both win."

EVE SHRUGGED into her medium-starch button-down blouse and buttoned it up over her lacy push-up bra. She pulled on and zipped boring khakis, effectively hiding the sheer lace panties that matched her bra. She'd deliberately picked the most nondescript outfit she'd brought along. She'd be damned if she'd have Jack think she'd dressed to entice him.

If he was still around. She'd needed a shower after arguably the most erotic sex she'd ever had. In retrospect, she wasn't sure if she'd started things rolling or if Jack had. Or if it had been more along the lines of a collaborative effort. She'd fail dismally on one of those word-association tests now. Strawberries. Sex. Chocolate. Sex. Champagne. Sex. Hollandaise sauce. Extraordinary orgasm.

She picked up the attaché case she'd brought in with her. She could care less whether she'd insulted him or not. She wasn't about to leave him in her room with access to her information while she showered and changed. She stepped out of the bathroom. Jack was still in her room. And despite herself, she was inordinately glad to see his smug, handsome self lolling about on the love seat with the towel back in place around his hips. God, she needed some kind of therapy if she could feel even a smidgen of attraction— much less this incredible tug—after this morning.

His assessing glance spoke volumes. He thought her outfit was dowdy. And deliberate. The musky scent of sex hung in the air, rendering her choice of outfit ridiculous. "I think I'll clean up a bit."

"Help yourself."

Jack disappeared into the bathroom.

Eve put her attaché in the closet and closed the door. She heard the shower come on in the bathroom and left the bedroom for the sitting room. She piled the dirty dishes on the tray and put it in the hallway outside the door. Just thinking about *that* left her weak kneed and distracted.

She wandered over to the window. The earlier driving downpour had slowed to a steady rain. The few people who'd ventured outside rushed along the sidewalk, huddled beneath umbrellas.

The shower cut off in the bathroom. Jack would be out soon. She, who was usually so decisive, couldn't decide whether she wanted Jack to stay or not. There were worse ways to spend a rainy day.

As if on cue, he walked into the room. He'd put on his running shorts and T-shirt, but his feet were bare, a fact she found very intimate and sexy. Apparently he didn't plan on going anywhere soon and actually she didn't mind.

She turned away from the window, fully expecting an awkwardness to settle between them. Instead, it was more of a companionship fraught with an undercurrent of sexual awareness. Not exactly cozy, but not uncomfortable either.

Without preamble, as if he'd rehearsed his speech in the shower, he said, "You claimed earlier the only thing you needed was this promotion. Why is it so important to you, Eve? I think there's more than blind ambition here." Jack took her spot at the window.

She preferred his bluntness to his practiced charm.

"Definitely." Eve bared her teeth in what her brothers referred to as her barracuda smile. "It's eyes-wide-open ambition."

Jack looked out the window and then turned to her again. "There's more to it than that."

"Obviously you want it badly as well. Why's it so important to you?" she countered. He had a way of asking very personal questions of others—well, of her at least—without offering up information on himself.

"I asked first."

"Why should I trust you with what's important to me?"

"Maybe you should ask yourself why you shouldn't? Is it going to affect the outcome? I don't think so." Jack shrugged in a very Gallic gesture.

"But why do you want to know?" She was dogging him, but Eve always needed to understand the *why* of the matter.

"Because I'm curious as to what makes you tick. Why do you want to know why I want the position?"

"Know thy enemy."

"And what if you discover you like me?"

"I'm willing to risk it." Much as she hated to concede it, Jack was right. What difference did it make if he knew why she wanted the promotion? It didn't give him an edge. She could explain her motivation all day, make love to him all night, and still come out on top. "My parents keep waiting on me to find a husband. To them my career is simply a stopgap on the way to matrimony. They don't outright disapprove as much as they tolerate my career—it's as if they're indulging a whim. I can still remember their disappointment when I finished college without my Mrs. degree." Surely if she had this promotion, they'd finally recognize her talent and hard work. And she'd feel as if she'd finally hit the mark. "I suppose it's a point of validation."

"Do you really think a promotion will change the way they see things?"

"Maybe. Maybe not." Besides, there was more than a measure of self-validation needed, as well. When you were the only one who believed in you, it was hard. And lonely. "There's only one way to know, though, isn't there? So, that's my big, bad motivation to winning. What about you, Jack? Why do you want this job so bad?"

Jack shifted from one foot to the other and then caught himself. So far, she'd seen very little that shook Jack up, outside of rock-the-Casbah sex. He was definitely more comfortable talking about Eve than himself. Which only whetted her curiosity.

"My family's fairly well-off. The LaRoux have traded in commercial property since San Francisco's gold-rush days."

Hmm. *Well-off* struck her as an understatement. She'd noticed the fine cut of his clothes, expensive watch, aforementioned boarding school and that arrogant air he wore so well. All of it screamed of a monied background.

"After summers spent at the office with my father and a couple of finance courses in college, I knew the family business wasn't for me."

"Because?" It sounded like a cushy job that carried a lot of power and nice paycheck. What was not to like?

Jack's smile had a cynical edge. "Commercial real estate bores me silly. But even more than that, when you step into a position, people assume it's not because you're good at what you do, but because of who you are. I wanted to prove I could be successful on my own. So—" he grinned, breathtakingly sexy with his beard darkening his jaw "—maybe this promotion is validation for me as well."

"How did your family take your decision?"

"It's been a point of contention." A bleakness about his eyes belied his smile and light tone.

Once again, she was fairly certain Jack had understated the case. Eve grudgingly admitted she admired Jack for walking away from a sure thing to prove himself. Dammit. She didn't want to like or admire anything about this man.

"Do you have any other siblings to run the family business?"

"My older brother Robert never thought of doing anything else. It's in his blood." Jack laughed in derision. "The business won't falter without me. It's all about control. My career choice takes me out of my father's realm of influence. And I might embarrass the family by not living up to the LaRoux reputation for success."

She also didn't want to know Jack had principles. It was so much easier to go for the jugular when you saw your competition as an unprincipled asshole. "Then I'd say we both have a lot riding on this promotion."

"I mean to have it, Eve." That same bleakness underscored his quiet declaration.

For the first time, with less than twenty-four hours before they met with Bill Bradley, Eve's unshakable faith in herself was shaken.

8

"WHAT DID YOU THINK?" Jack asked as they rode the elevator down from Bradley Enterprises' sixteenth-floor office suite. Even though they stood a professional distance apart, Eve's light, fresh scent tantalized him in the confined space.

What he really wanted to know was if Eve had gone commando to the meeting. She'd taunted him with it Friday night, well, technically early Saturday morning. The question had never been far from his mind throughout the entire meeting.

The elevator chimed and stopped on the tenth floor to take on passengers.

"I'll let you know what I thought later," she murmured. A group that looked as if they'd just concluded their own meeting, pushed in. Eve moved closer to Jack to make room. The curve of her buttock, the sexy line of her back, the exposed nape of her neck, her clean scent—all of them set his body on red alert. It was almost more arousing to have her so near, yet not touching him.

There were two additional stops, allowing more passengers and causing her arm, shoulder and hip to press intimately against him. Okay, so maybe having her touch him was more arousing. But there was nothing provocative in her touch. They were wedged in the back corner like sardines in a can. But all Jack could think about, with her pressed against him and her scent a part of every breath he drew, was what had happened the last time they'd shared an elevator. His heart pounded like a jackhammer. Walking out of the confined space sporting a hard-on would be beyond embarrassing. Jack forced himself to imagine losing the vice presidency to counteract Eve's disruptive effect on his body.

Finally. The elevator opened to the atrium lobby and Eve's soft, rounded, tempting behind was mercifully no longer in close proximity to his crotch. For a man who lived in a state of perpetual detachment, he'd come perilously close to breaking out in a sweat.

She strode across the lobby, her heels clicking against the marble floor, confident and totally oblivious to the jackass in the Brooks Brothers suit leaning against the wall and craning his neck to check her out. She was oblivious, but Jack didn't miss it. It should've amused him. Instead, it annoyed him.

By the time he'd paused to glare down the other guy and then proceeded out the revolving front door, Eve had a cab waiting at the curb. She was one of the most competent women he'd ever met.

Jack climbed into the back seat with her and closed the door, giving the driver their hotel name. Eve faced him in the cab's stale interior.

"Bill Bradley's a sexist pig. I kept waiting for him to ask me to fetch coffee." Eve shrugged, more amused than offended. Was it because her family held a similar attitude? He thought it highly likely.

"I wasn't sure what you'd do the first time he called you *little lady*," he said, smiling. "Bradley's a dinosaur if he doesn't recognize your talent." Great sex aside, Jack thought Eve was a smart, funny lady who was extremely talented.

She widened her eyes in mocking surprise. "Did you just give me a compliment?"

"Damn, I did. What was I thinking?"

"Are you going soft on me, Jack?"

He leaned into the space separating them until he saw himself reflected in the crystalline depths of her eyes. "Eve, I don't think I'm capable of being anything but hard when I'm around you."

"I suppose I asked for that very distracting thought."

"I suppose you did."

"Okay, forget I went there. Bradley *is* a dinosaur. But at least he's a self-aware dinosaur. That's why he needs us. To get him up to speed and try to recoup some of the market share he's lost. He would've probably taken you to a high-end strip joint for lunch if I hadn't been there."

She was frighteningly insightful. Jack guessed not much escaped Eve. Except, according to Nev's office gossip source, her boyfriend who did her secretary. "He suggested we go this afternoon after I dropped you at the hotel."

"What time are you getting together?" She glanced out the cab's window. To a casual observer, she appeared to care less. But he was getting to know this woman. He felt the tension beneath the calm.

"We're not."

"What?" She turned her head sharply toward him.

He had her attention now. "I told him there wasn't enough time before my flight left."

"You don't fly out until early evening."

He raised a brow in inquiry. How did she know when he flew out?

"I checked your itinerary when I checked mine," she said, without embarrassment. "But tell me, why did you pass up the opportunity to boy bond while you stuff dollars into G-strings? It'd definitely give you the competitive edge. I think it falls into the wining and dining category."

"For the same reason you didn't show a little more leg or give Bradley a special smile to gain the competitive edge. I doubt he's immune to a pretty face and a hot body." In pumps and an above-the-knee skirt, her legs seemed to go on forever. Their buddy Bradley had noticed as well, without Eve trying to attract his attention.

"I don't consider myself either."

"Trust me. You're both." After all she'd wrecked his equilibrium, usually rock steady, from the moment he'd seen her.

"I'm not sure whether I'm flattered or insulted. Don't brains count for anything with you men?"

"Opt for flattered. A pretty face, hot body and brains aren't mutually exclusive."

"Not that I'd trade on sex, but that third one's a deal

buster for Bradley. I'd guess he prefers his women without a lot of brains. But you still haven't said why you aren't joining the good old boys club."

"I prefer my women naked in private, without an audience. And I'm not joining the good old boys club because I don't need to." He'd infinitely prefer to spend the next few hours with *her*. Naked.

She didn't try to mask her disbelief.

"What's the matter, Eve? Surprised I have scruples?"

"Actually, yes. You have a reputation for being ruthless."

"Ruthless doesn't mean unethical. And I told you, Eve. Remember that night at the pool? Remember the chemistry? That wasn't about Hendley and Wells." He turned to her but didn't touch her. Not yet. "Just like this isn't about Hendley and Wells." He kissed her. "Or the Bradley account." He kissed her again. "Or the vice presidency." Their lips clung in a slow, thorough exploration. Until the cab hit a pothole, jarring them both back to reality.

Eve leaned away from him and smoothed a nonexistent stray hair back into the twist at her nape. "Jack, we need to talk."

In his experience, those words and that tone were not a positive sign. "Okay."

"It's not going to do either one of us any good if this gets around the office."

She really had the most abysmal opinion of him. And he shouldn't give a damn. But he did. "I don't kiss and tell, Eve."

"No need to get in a snit, Jack. I obviously have more to lose than you do if word gets around that we slept together. You'd be a stud and I'd be easy. Plain and simple. The corporate double standard is alive and well."

"I can keep *my* mouth shut. Women are the ones who have to share things with their girlfriends," he said, striking back.

"I think I can manage to keep your sexual prowess to myself."

Jack's cell phone rang. He glanced at caller ID. Neville. He flipped open the phone. "Hi, Nev. I'm on my way back to the hotel. Did media get the Abrahms project wrapped up?"

"It looks good. I'll e-mail the changes to you. Now, don't leave me hanging. How'd it go with Bradley? Do you have any fabulous ideas knocking around already? Was Evil Eve a total bitch in the meeting? How did Bradley take it when she blew in on her broomstick?"

Jack winced. The phone was essentially between him and Eve. Nev was enthusiastic. Translate—loud. Eve held out one hand, palm up, expectant. Nev had just blown it...and Eve held a black belt. Jack decided he wasn't taking Nev's heat. He handed her the phone.

"Neville was it?" she asked with saccharin sweetness.

"Yes." Jack heard the choked, one-syllable, one-word response.

"I'm afraid my broomstick's in the shop, so I resorted to a taxi. But, for the record, I prefer Eve the Avenger. And I tried to keep my bitchiness at bay—it makes a better impression on the client, don't you think? I'm giving you back to Jack now, but please let me know if there's anything else I can clear up for you."

EVE SLICED through the water, seeking the mindless-ness of swimming laps. She found the rhythm.

Stroke, kick, breathe.

Stroke, kick, breathe.

But the serenity eluded her.

Jack's swim invitation, after he'd explored her lack of undergarments, seemed like a good idea at the time. Now it was merely a distraction.

She was far too aware of him keeping pace with her, ridiculously cognizant of his lean form next to her. Even through the water, she could feel his attraction, the magnetism that drew her to him.

And despite her better judgment, she *was* drawn to him. She should be thinking about their earlier meet-ing with Bill Bradley. Ideas should be randomly filter-ing through her head while she swam. That would be the smart thing to do. Instead, she was remembering the feel and taste of Jack's mouth, the tensile strength of his body beneath hers as they found release in each other, the heady scent of his expensive aftershave that lingered on her skin after he'd gone.

She finished her laps and hoisted herself up the side and out of the pool, frustrated with her lack of self-control and with Jack's power to wreck her concentration. Was this part of his plan? To seduce her into senselessness? He might not hang out at a strip club to press a competitive advantage. Once again, he'd managed to impress her. She hated to admit how glad she was that he didn't want to sit around and watch nubile eighteen-year-olds wrap themselves around a phallicly symbolic pole—but she didn't put it above him to take advantage of this attraction between them.

So if she was going to be distracted by him, she'd make sure she sent him home in the same shape.

Jack climbed out of the pool, water sluicing down his body. He slicked his hair back with both hands. Eve tossed him a towel from the stack provided by the hotel.

"Thanks." He caught it with one hand.

"Jack."

"Eve?"

"I have two hours before I have to catch a cab for the airport." She leaned forward to blot the water from her legs.

His eyes darkened and his gaze scorched her. "Two hours is a long time. I could help you dry off. You know I'm good at finding wet spots," he said wriggling his eyebrows.

His playfulness took Eve by surprise and she laughed aloud. "You are very good at that. But how many times does that line work and how many times have you gotten your face slapped?"

Jack dried his shoulders and looked distinctly uncomfortable. "I didn't mean for it to come out that way. You had missed a spot drying off and I didn't think before I spoke."

Well. "You don't strike me as a spontaneous kind of guy."

"That's me. Mr. Spur-of-the-moment."

She recognized tongue-in-cheek when she heard it. "Right."

"So, my offer still stands." He grasped the ends of the towel draped around her neck and pulled her into his personal space. Close enough that she could see the fine sheen of moisture caught on his skin and the errant droplets of water in the dark hair bisecting his belly. He took his own towel and dragged it along her neck, down her chest, the backs of his fingers whispering fire along her skin. "See how good I am at drying you off."

"Your technique is flawless, but I'm still very wet."

"Perhaps we should continue in your room. I can also help you pack."

"That's a generous offer."

"I'm feeling expansive," he said.

"Really? That was just what I had in mind."

"The way I see it, this is the last stop on that round-trip ticket to paradise."

She nodded. They were both well aware that this was the end of the line for their fling. "I believe you're right about that."

"My flight leaves after yours. Why don't you call and see if you can reschedule yours for a later time."

"Why would I want to do that?" she teased him.

"Why wouldn't you want to do that?"

"Hmm. Perhaps I need to be convinced."

"I'm prepared to fully, thoroughly convince you. But once I get started, you'll wind up missing that flight anyway."

"AND THEY SAY the traffic is bad in New York," Eve said.

The cab finally pulled curbside at Chicago's O'Hare terminal. Jack hadn't been too sure they'd make their respective flights, especially since they'd lost track of time earlier. He checked his watch. They should be okay.

They got out of the cab and Jack paid the cabbie, pocketing the receipt.

Eve, all business in her black suit and pumps, pulled her small suitcase behind her. She was vastly different from the naked woman screaming his name in a rush of orgasmic passion less than an hour ago. He found both faces of Eve equally fascinating. Eve the Temptress and Eve the Coolheaded Business Woman.

"I'm not sure if I know any women who could pack an entire weekend in that small suitcase," he said as they entered the terminal.

"There are plenty of us around. I told you. You're just used to those high-maintenance women you surround yourself with."

Carol Ann, his last girlfriend, would've needed the pull-along for her makeup and skin care alone. They'd spent a weekend together in Tahoe and she'd brought along a small suitcase full of cream, lotions and makeup.

"That's a distinct possibility. I may have to reconsider my taste in women."

"And I think that's highly implausible."

Eve had been an anomaly—a taste of something different. A taste he could definitely get used to.

She paused before the departure board and checked her flight number against the neon information. "I'm at Gate three. What about you?"

Jack reminded himself he was grateful for her cool professionalism. What had he expected, for her to cling, suggest he call or fly out for a visit? Hell, no. Here it was, the end of their sensual voyage. Time to switch tracks.

He scanned the board. "I'm at the opposite end of the terminal."

She held out a slim hand, "It's been...interesting, Jack." Her eyes, those remarkable translucent pools, were cool and fathomless. The way she was acting, the past few days might not have even happened.

To hell with a handshake. He wanted one more glimpse of the other Eve. "Yes, it has been."

His carry-on and attaché slid to the ground as he bypassed her extended hand and pulled her into his arms, melding his mouth to hers, tasting her, absorbing her one last time. He cradled her head in his hands, his lips memorizing the contour of hers.

Finally the kiss ended. Eve bent and retrieved her laptop and carry-on.

"Have a safe trip, Jack."

She turned and walked away, leaving Jack standing at the terminal junction. The crowd soon swallowed her and he was left feeling slightly foolish. He was usually the one who walked away. This was new territory.

He slung his bag and the laptop over his shoulder, then lost himself in the airport chaos. When Jack arrived at his gate, the flight was already boarding. Thank goodness. He hated sitting around waiting.

He handed over his flight info at the ticket counter for confirmation.

"Oh, I'm sorry, Mr. LaRoux, but this seat is already taken. Here's your new seat. Have a nice trip." The redhead smiled warmly at him as he joined the boarding queue.

The return flight to San Francisco was packed. He glanced again at his boarding pass as he shuffled along the narrow aisle. He scanned ahead to 26B. Great. Just great. He'd been bumped from business to coach—and he was in a middle seat to boot.

He eyed the tight quarters and stowed his two bags in the overhead compartment. Forget working in this tight space. He wasn't exactly sure how he was going to manage to squeeze himself in.

"Excuse me."

Jack climbed over the large man who easily spilled into two seats and settled between Mr. Jumbo and a kid clutching a barf bag. That was a very bad sign.

"Can I get your mom for you?" he asked the pale, freckle-faced boy scrunched next to the window.

Maybe Mom would want to trade seats with Jack to be with her son.

The boy shook his head, a picture of queasy misery. "I'm flying to my dad's."

The plane hadn't even taxied down the runway yet. What would happen if they hit a patch of turbulence? Poor kid. Poor Jack.

On his left, Muscle-man-gone-to-fat glared at Jack, even as his right arm and massive thigh crowded into Jack's space. Shit.

The plane backed out onto the tarmac and the flight attendants began their spiel. Jack closed his eyes and tried to block out his surroundings, willing himself to focus on the Bradley campaign. Instead, images of Eve filled his head. Angry Eve. Seductive Eve. Laughing Eve. Aloof Eve.

Beneath him, his chair vibrated as another kid behind him kicked the back of his seat. Again and again and again.

The plane picked up speed and the front wheels lifted. The kid beside him puked. No way he was opening his eyes to make sure the kid hadn't missed the bag. He didn't want to know.

Welcome to the plane trip from hell.

EVE SETTLED into the oversize, first-class seat. The plane had been packed to capacity except for first-class and she'd been upgraded to this seat. The stewardess offered a complimentary glass of champagne.

"Thanks," she murmured, and helped herself. She took a sip, enjoying the feel of the cool liquid sliding down her throat. Chilled champagne and Jack's hot mouth. Instant, erotic association. No doubt Jack was sitting in first-class, knocking back a Scotch, having charmed the attendant with a smile and a droll comment. Which beautifully illustrated why having a relationship with a gorgeous, arrogant, charming man like Jack would be lunacy. Because a woman wouldn't even have to wonder when she wasn't with Jack. She'd know. She'd know without a doubt that other women were coming on to him.

By God, she wasn't going to sit here making herself feel bad. Just because they'd had a weekend of fabulous sex didn't mean she had to sit around mooning over him.

She'd put this time to good use. And thinking about Jack didn't qualify. She'd work on the ad campaign. She pulled out the attaché and pulled out her laptop and a sheaf of neatly scripted notes. Except it wasn't *her* laptop or *her* notes. For several heartbeats she forgot to breathe.

She had Jack's briefcase and laptop. And that meant he had hers. And if she was staring at his campaign notes, he was staring at hers.

Or maybe they were bogus notes to throw her off track.

Had that a-handshake-isn't-enough kiss merely been a ruse? Had he deliberately distracted her so she wouldn't notice when he picked up her bag?

Damn his black soul to hell for the fact that she couldn't trust him—and that he'd reduced her to the point that it actually mattered to her.

She glanced again at the sheaf of papers. It'd been one thing to announce she didn't need to cheat to win, but it was a different matter altogether with his notes in her hand.

Just how important was this promotion to her again?

9

JACK DROPPED his bags inside his front door and made a beeline to the kitchen for a glass of water and some ibuprofen. He had a motherlode of a headache. Of course, the kid who had puked until he was having dry heaves probably felt infinitely worse.

Jack washed down the tablets and closed his eyes, rubbing his temples, willing the pounding to subside. After three days of sharing a hotel room with Eve, the solitude of his condo should soothe him. Instead, it simply felt empty. His cell phone chirped and he reached into his pocket.

He flipped it open. "Hi, Nev."

"Are you alone? Is the coast clear? You're not going to let me insult someone and then hand me over to be strung up again, are you?"

Apparently Nev planned to bitch about that for another week or so. "I'm home. Alone. What do you need?"

"Terse, are we?"

"I've got a headache." And dammit, if he didn't know better, he might think he was suffering from symptoms of withdrawal—from Eve.

"You should've taken my advice and got laid. It would've cured what ails you—"

"I did get laid and I still have a headache." Eve had been both the cure and the cause.

"So, sue me if it wasn't good."

"What do you need, Nev?" Jack was running short on patience.

"I need for you to check and tell me which version of the Abrahms proposal you have."

"I'm sure I have whatever version you e-mailed to me."

"Well, you need to check. There was a mix-up on the graphics and I know you need to review this tonight for tomorrow afternoon's presentation."

"Okay, hang on a sec." Jack picked up his briefcase and placed it on the table. Propping the cell phone against his shoulder, he unzipped the case and pulled out his laptop. Dammit, his headache wasn't any better and where were his handwritten notes? He shoved his hand back into the case, feeling around, a knot forming in the pit of his stomach. He pulled out a zippered notepad and a small clear plastic cosmetic case containing one lipstick tube, a tampon, and a half-eaten chocolate bar with a raspberry center. Goddammit. He closed his eyes. "Eve has my briefcase. I picked up hers."

"You did what?" Neville's sopranic squeal sliced through his already pounding head.

"We shared a cab to the airport. The cases must've gotten switched then." It was close enough to the truth. Neville was far too perceptive. Neither Jack nor Eve needed Nev guessing at just how far their acquaintance had gone.

"Jaaack. This is not good. Evil Eve probably did this on purpose."

"No." He'd been the one who grabbed her. "I think it was an honest mistake."

"Are you telling me you trust her?"

"Well, there's trust, and then there's trust," he said, paraphrasing the woman in question. "I don't believe she deliberately switched them, but I don't believe she's above looking through my notes." She'd talked a good game, but he'd seen the look in her eyes, the determination on her face when she'd talked about winning the campaign.

"What're we going to do? We have to do something, Jack."

"It looks as if I'm flying to New York and back."

"That'll cost a fortune and you'll be exhausted for the meeting."

Jack checked his watch. "Her plane hasn't landed yet. Chances are she had the same return trip from hell that I did and never got a chance to open her briefcase either. If I call her and tell her, well, then I've told her and she knows what she has. As it is, she might not know. Hopefully, I can show up before she realizes what happened." This had absolutely nothing to do with seeing her again. This was all about protecting his work and his shot at the vice presidency. It was simply a business decision made by a calculating man.

"Or she could've already gone through your files and made copies of everything."

"I guess that's a chance I'll have to take." He figured his odds were fifty-fifty.

For a second silence reigned. Having worked together for so long, Jack knew Nev was digesting the full impact of the situation. This could bury their chances of getting the vice presidency and Jack knew that Nev had as much at stake as he did.

"How can I help? What do you need for me to do?"

"Get me on the next available to New York. I'll take a cab to the airport and you can call me on the way with the flight info. Then you'll have to track down Eve's home address."

"Are you going to tell her you're coming?"

Essentially, Neville wanted to know if he was willing to tip his hand. "No. I'm not going to call her."

"Excellent. I'll get on the phone with the airline."

"Thanks, Nev. Catch me on my cell when you have a flight."

"Okay. Jack?"

"Yes?"

"You realize there's no way you'll ever know for sure if she went through your files. I trust you'll take good notes when you read through hers on the flight."

EVE SQUINTED at the clock. Why was the alarm going off at four in the morning? She reached out and slapped at the top of the clock, but the buzzing persisted.

Oh. It was her buzzer. She stumbled out of bed and across the room to the intercom speaker. If another drunk had managed to get past Antony the doorman, she wasn't going to be a happy camper. "Yes?"

"Eve. It's me, Jack."

"Jack who?"

"How many of us do you know? Jack LaRoux."

Okay. It was four in the morning. Jack should've been home hours ago and instead he was downstairs. In New York. "Why aren't you in San Francisco?"

"Can I come up for this discussion?"

"Sure." She buzzed him through and dashed for the bathroom to get in as much damage control as possible.

She snatched up the toothbrush and brushed her teeth, dragged a brush through her hair and scrubbed at the mascara that had settled in the fine lines beneath her eyes. That would teach her to go to bed without washing her face first. She'd been exhausted when she got home and had pretty much fallen into bed. But it didn't make for a pretty sight now.

A quiet knock sounded at her door. She sprinted across the room and checked the peephole before sliding open the three locks and taking off the chain.

She opened the door and let him in.

Jack looked like hell. His hair stood on end, his jaw sported more than a hint of five-o'clock shadow, his eyes were bloodshot, and his usual impeccable attire was definitely askew, with one edge of his shirttail almost hanging out. And even so, her knees were none too steady and she felt the heat standing near him seemed to bring on. He looked wonderful.

Was she sleepwalking? Or having some weird soon-to-be erotic dream? "Jack?"

He stood stock-still, his eyes raking her. If she was dreaming, she thought it a good move she'd brushed her teeth in her dream. "Eve."

She had no idea if he reached for her, or if she reached for him, or if it was a mutual moment. But within seconds, she was back in Jack's arms, breathing his scent, feeling the rush of his breath and the brush of his lips against her hair. And then his mouth was on hers and if this was a dream, it was one of the best damn dreams she'd ever had. She really didn't want to wake up anytime soon. Especially since she was dreaming in full sensory experience, well aware of the press of his hard body against hers, his scent that wrapped around her, the heat invading her body, the dampness gathering between her thighs.

Eve didn't waste another second, afraid she'd wake up before she found the satisfaction she craved. She tugged his shirt the rest of the way out of his trousers and plied her fingers against the muscled plane of his belly. It was like striking a match to kindling.

Jack kissed her harder, deeper. She smoothed his jacket over his shoulders, walking him backward toward her bed. For once, she appreciated the limited floor space of her studio apartment. They tumbled onto the mattress together. She tugged his shirt over his head while he shed his trousers and underwear.

And then his hands and his mouth were on her breasts, driving her to the verge of madness.

For a second Jack fumbled and she realized he was sheathing himself. And then he parted her thighs, his fingers finding and testing her slick heat.

"Yes," she urged him on and in.

He entered her and she thrust upward, filling herself with him. Eve wrapped her legs around his lean hips, driving him harder. She was on fire for him. Frantic with need, she matched his rhythm with her own, seeking the release only he could bring.

"Eve, Eve, Eve," he called her name as she shuddered and bucked against him. Jack collapsed beside her on the bed.

When her last spasm subsided and her breathing slowed to something close to normal, Eve pinched herself. Ouch. Yeah, she was definitely awake. She didn't dare do that earlier in case she really was still asleep.

"Now that was what I call a hello." Jack nuzzled her temple, his hand splayed against her naked belly.

Eve rolled to her side and propped herself on her hand. The light filtering through the curtains silhouetted his profile. "As good as it was, I don't imagine you flew all the way from California for that." The foolish part of her that she'd never admit to anyone, the romantic who died a small death every time she managed to make another bad man decision, secretly hoped that it might be so. "Why are you here at four in the morning, Jack?"

"Our briefcases were switched at the airport. I didn't realize until I got home."

Uh-huh. "I found out on the plane."

"Why didn't you call me?"

Did she detect a note of accusation in his tone?

"I couldn't call until my flight landed. Hendley and Wells was closed and I don't have your number. I was going to call in the morning." And really, after several complimentary glasses of champagne on the plane, she hadn't much cared by the time she got home. Another thought occurred to her. "How did you know where I live?"

"Nev tracked down the information for me."

"My buddy, Neville. What'd he do? Call information for the nearest coven?"

Jack ignored her sarcasm. "I don't know how he got your address. I didn't ask."

"So you flew across the country to wake me up and tell me I had your briefcase?"

"Pretty much." He shifted on her sheets and she thought it was guilt that had his oh-so-fine behind moving. "I have a meeting tomorrow afternoon— well, this afternoon, and I needed some of the information on my laptop."

"You expect me to believe Neville the hyper-efficient Nazi doesn't have everything on your computer backed up? Try another one. You came because you didn't trust me not to looks at yours, didn't you?" She jumped up and pulled her nightgown down over her thighs. She was such an idiot. Jumping his bones like that when he'd really only wanted his briefcase. The sex must've been a bonus.

Jack stood as well and shrugged, looking like some displaced Roman god in the light filtering through the window. "I wasn't sure whether you knew yet or not. I thought I'd come and we could exchange bags. I have to catch a cab in an hour and a half to make my flight back."

Eve snapped on the bedside lamp. Roman god her ass. He was just another naked opportunist. Jack pulled on his briefs and then his pants.

Eve crossed to the kitchen table that doubled as a computer stand and picked up his attaché case. He was tucking in his shirt when she turned. She resisted the urge to whack him with it. Instead, she dropped it on the mattress.

"Here's your briefcase. You'll just have to get to the airport early, because we don't have an hour and a half worth of business left between us."

"Eve—"

"There's nothing else to say, Jack," she interrupted him.

Jack pulled a card out of his briefcase. He scribbled something on the back of it and placed it on her nightstand. "There's my home and cell number if you need to get in touch with me." He slung the briefcase strap over his shoulder.

She didn't spare the card a glance. "I won't need to contact you."

Jack walked to the door without saying anything else.

"Aren't you going to ask me if I read them, Jack?" she asked.

He turned to face her. "You never asked me, did you?"

She had assumed that given the opportunity, he'd read through her notes. She didn't have to answer the question. He knew it had been rhetorical.

"That's what I thought." His smile was full of cynicism. He slipped the chain and opened the door. "Bye, Eve."

10

"WE'VE GOT A DECISION to make. LaRoux had access to my files—our briefcases got mixed up at the airport. My preliminary ideas for expanding to include the female market were only reinforced when we met with Bill Bradley. It's definitely a growing segment he's overlooked. I think this idea is a winner. But chances are LaRoux has seen it." Eve leaned back in the chair and glanced at her team members gathered around the "war table." As account executive she didn't have to put it up for consensus. She could dictate the direction and they'd have to follow. But through sheer idiocy and carelessness, she'd compromised the most important project they'd ever undertaken. True, she was the one who stood to gain a vice presidency, but every member of her team would be recognized and their status affected accordingly. "So, we're a team here. Do we scrap this idea and go back to the drawing board or do we roll with it?"

Deb Weymouth, her media specialist, spoke up, the light of battle gleaming in her eyes. "I say we teach LaRoux a thing or two. Namely that we can outshine him and his pathetic wannabes, even if he knows our plan."

"I don't know that he actually *looked* at my notes, Deb. I only know he had access to them."

"Did you sneak a peek at his outline, Eve?" Andrea asked.

She'd never been so tempted in her life. Moral decisions were much more difficult when you actually had to stare down an opportunity. Especially when no one would've been the wiser. Except her. She'd read the first paragraph and stopped, knowing she still had to live with herself. "Once I realized I had his notes, I put them away. We don't need to cheat to win."

"Wouldn't it be considered a competitive advantage?" The question came from LaTonya.

"It felt enough like cheating to me."

"But cheating would be—"

Eve felt control of the meeting slipping away. "Okay, we're not here to split hairs over semantics. Let's put it to a vote. Who wants to go with what we have?"

"Screw LaRoux, let's roll." Darren, full of British piss and vinegar, and covered in tattoos, had a potty mouth but was a true genius with a camera.

To a person, everyone jumped onboard. Eve released a breath she hadn't realized she'd been holding. Pleased with her team's decision, they spent the next half hour frameworking her idea and another hour brainstorming various approaches. The meeting concluded and everyone left, psyched but enthused. All except Andrea, that is.

"Let's grab some lunch," Andrea said, a quirky expression on her face.

Eve really didn't feel up to dealing with her friend. She'd tossed and turned after Jack left, and she had finally given up the idea of sleep. She needed more than three hours' rest to function like a real human being. "I would, but I have to tie up some loose ends on the Sherwood project. They're in for the dog-and-pony show tomorrow."

"Good. You can do that after lunch."

She definitely wasn't up for lunch when Andrea was in this mood. "Maybe tomorrow—"

Andrea held up her hand. It must be serious business. "We need to talk and, trust me, you'd rather talk outside of the office. Your choice. But we're talking, Sunshine."

"Okay." Eve closed her laptop with a snap. She didn't know what was so damned important that Andrea had to speak to her. But she'd soon find out. "Let's do lunch."

An uneasy silence hung between them as they left the building and picked up sandwiches at the corner deli. Well, Andrea picked up a sandwich. Eve picked up a container of overpriced romaine and lemon juice. She wasn't particularly hungry, having devoured a chocolate bar just before the meeting. Dammit, she couldn't even enjoy chocolate any more without thinking of Jack licking the sticky sweet off of her. And she didn't want to think about that. It had been fun and it was over. End of trip. Destination done.

"So, what's on your mind that's so important, Sunshine?" She threw the nickname back at Andrea. They were friends, but she didn't particularly appreciate Andrea's strong-arm tactics.

"You slept with him, didn't you?"

Eve was glad they were already sitting. Andrea's question took her by surprise.

"I'd have to know who he is before I can answer that question."

"Jack the Ripper is your mystery man, isn't he?"

How could Andrea have possibly figured it out? Eve played dumb. "Why would you say that?"

"Your face gave it away when we were in that meeting."

Eve kept her features schooled. "What about my face?"

"You're doing it again. You don't have any expression on your face. Every time we've ever talked about Mr. Yumm-o, you've always had this faint sneer. Just a look of general dislike. I know that expression you're wearing now and it means you're hiding something. And I think you're hiding Jack."

Eve slumped against the park bench. She was tired and frustrated and damn Jack to hell, she did need to talk to her girlfriend about it. "Don't sound so judgmental. You were the one who recommended a fling."

"But not with Jack the Ripper." Andrea slapped her forehead with her hand. "You really know how to pick 'em, girlfriend."

"Thanks. That's making me feel one-hundred-percent better."

"You weren't going to tell me, were you?" She looked hurt.

Andrea was one of the first people Eve had met when she'd moved to New York. They'd become firm, fast friends and as a rule, they didn't keep secrets from each other. She'd wanted to tell Andrea. "No. I wanted to but you have such an expressive face and if this gets out...well, it wouldn't do either one of us any good."

"Well, if you had to fling with LaRoux, please tell me it was good."

"No."

"No? You're kidding. Please tell me you're kidding."

"It wasn't good. It was great."

"Now that's more like it. Is he as yumm-o as I've heard?"

Desire rippled through her, remembering exactly how yumm-o he was. "More. Dark hair. Nice clothes. A sense of humor. Most gorgeous men take themselves so seriously they can't laugh at themselves, but not Jack."

"Are we talking about Jack the Ripper or Saint Jack?"

Heat crawled up Eve's neck. "Jack's definitely no saint."

"Well, that's good. Who wants a saint in the bedroom?"

For a moment she lost herself in the memories of the explosive chemistry between her and Jack.

Andrea waved her hand in front of Eve's face. "Hello. So it was that good?"

Eve didn't miss the wistful note in Andrea's voice.

Andrea had the heart of a romantic and if Eve wasn't careful, her friend would be blowing her interlude with Jack way out of proportion. But she wasn't going to lie.

"Better than good. But don't forget he conveniently didn't introduce himself."

"Do you think he was setting you up?"

"He says not, but he probably was. He's absolutely gorgeous and I'm not." She felt supremely foolish recounting this to Andrea.

"You're not exactly a dog."

"Thanks, but we're talking head-turning, heart-thumping, chick-magnet gorgeous." Eve abandoned all pretense of eating her spartan Caesar salad and gave Andrea the abbreviated version of her weekend with Jack, finishing up with his early morning visit.

"Baby girl! When you fling, by God, you fling. You mean, he came in and you had your wicked way with him this morning before he went back to the airport? Awesome."

"Until I found out he was there because he thought I'd plunder through his files."

"Eve, Eve, Eve. You knew the bags were switched. How were you going to handle it?"

"I thought we could overnight them."

"Exactly. And when you factor in that men are basically lazy, like they're not gonna do anything more than they absolutely have to...well, it seems to me that Jack was looking for a reason to show up at your place."

Eve only barely refrained from clapping her hands

over her ears the way she used to when her brothers had teased her as a child. She absolutely did not want to hear this. Her heart didn't need to believe Jack was anything more than an adversary seeking an advantage. "Let's not romanticize any of this. That would be supremely foolish."

"Most women wouldn't think so."

"Andrea, you just don't understand. You'd have to meet him. He should come with a warning label."

"Are you trying to convince me or yourself?"

"YOU'RE DIFFERENT." Nev cocked his head to one side, studying Jack from the other side of his sleek black desk.

"Try tired."

"No. You're exhausted after every major presentation, so that's nothing new. It's something I can't quite put my finger on." Neville pursed his lips and tapped his finger against his cheek.

Jack felt like a zoo exhibit. "Perhaps you'd like to put up a piece of glass and charge admission."

"You are *so* not in a better mood than when you left. Of course, if I had to share a cab with Awful Eve and then fly across America the Beautiful to exchange laptops with her, I suppose I'd be in a piss as well."

"She's not so bad." Jack leaned back in his chair.

"Please. Do not even tell me that I just heard she's not so bad."

"Actually, if you hadn't insulted her within hearing distance—"

"My psychic abilities were on the fritz. How was I supposed to know she was right there?"

Nev was going to begrudge that ad nauseam. "A little reserve now and then wouldn't be out of line. But as I was saying, if the two of you hadn't gotten off to a bad start, I think you'd like her. She's smart and outspoken and sometimes downright rude—just your type of girl."

"If I liked girls," Nev said with an arch smile. "Now, you can't just throw out that tidbit and not tell me what Her Awfulness said that was so rude."

"She said I was needy." Damn her to hell. That comment was driving him crazy. He hadn't planned on saying anything to Nev, but he figured Nev knew him as well as anyone and was the perfect candidate to refute her. Plus, Nev pretty much thought the same as a woman.

Nev, uninvited, dropped into a chair. "Oh, my."

"Ridiculous, isn't it?"

"I'd say insightful. Especially based on one meeting and a cab ride." Suspicion narrowed Neville's eyes. "Exactly how much time did you spend with her?"

"She flew in early. We ran into one another at the pool. She swims and she drinks Scotch."

He was definitely slow-witted this morning. He'd been so busy answering Nev's question, it just registered with him that far from refuting her, Nev had agreed with her. "And what the hell do you mean 'how insightful.' Wrong answer, Nev."

For a split second, Nev hesitated, as if unsure how to proceed. Then he drew in a deep breath and reverted to his usual brash, bold self. "You are needy, Jack."

Jack rubbed his brow. He was obviously losing his mind if he'd brought that up to Neville. And he was not needy. Needy described the poor slobs who'd cried under their covers at night at boarding school because their parents didn't visit. He'd made damn sure, at an early age, that he wasn't needy.

"Forget I mentioned it." Jack reached for the file on his desk, clearly dismissing both Nev and the conversation.

Except Nev had no intention of being dismissed. "You need to be the best and have the best. Like you're trying to fill up some empty well inside you."

"This discussion is closed." Jack didn't glance up from the paper.

"You keep everyone at a distance. You only let me close to you, because I bulldog you."

Jack was tired, out of sorts, and he'd had enough. "What part of *the discussion is closed* didn't you understand?"

Neville sniffed, "Well, I was only making the point—"

He'd had enough of Eve and Nev's "points" and "insights" to last a lifetime. Jack stood, pointed at the door and shouted, "Go. Out. Now."

Nev left, casting a shame-on-you glance at Jack before he closed the door behind him.

And the devil of the matter was that he was ashamed. Jack didn't lose his temper. Ever. Quite frankly he didn't know what in the hell was happening to him.

Not only did he feel like a zoo exhibit, but one whose cage had been thoroughly rattled.

EVE LOOKED UP at the knock on her door. She'd been engrossed in reviewing the Sherwood account, a new client she'd snatched from a formidable competitor, The Dean Group. She should be excited at such a prestigious win. Today, however, she was generally irritable and further agitated by the interruption. "Yes?"

LaTonya poked her head around the door. "You have a delivery."

Well, then why the heck didn't she just bring it in since she'd already interrupted Eve's train of thought? "Okay."

LaTonya's head disappeared. Eve rolled her neck, stretching her muscles, trying to dispel some of her tension. She was not short-tempered today because she missed Jack. She didn't miss Jack. She missed *sex* with Jack. Any woman in her right mind would miss extraordinary sex. A woman could fall into bed with half-a-dozen men, maybe an even dozen, and not find sex as good as it had been with Jack.

The door swung inward and LaTonya reappeared, carrying a shrink-wrapped basket tied at the top with an elaborate velvet ribbon edged in gold. "This just came. I knew you were busy, but..."

She plopped the basket onto Eve's desk and waited expectantly. It wasn't Eve's birthday. She hadn't gotten a promotion—yet. Hendley and Wells didn't allow corporate gift giving. That meant it was personal and she wasn't opening a personal gift in front of LaTonya.

"Thanks."

"You're welcome." LaTonya stood rooted to the spot. "There wasn't a card. I checked for you. I thought you'd want me to."

"Thank you. I appreciate it. If you'll hold my calls for a few minutes, I'll let you know if I need anything else."

"You're not going to open it?"

LaTonya wasn't winning any professionalism awards. But then again, at least she hadn't spanked the monkey on Eve's desktop like Delores and Perry, Eve reasoned, in an attempt to view her glass as half full as opposed to half empty. "I am. When you leave."

"Oh, okay. Just let me know if you need anything."

"I promise, I will."

The door closed behind her and Eve looked at the basket for a long moment without opening it. The up-thrust neck of a champagne bottle was unmistakable. She'd give three guesses as to the sender and the first two didn't count. She tugged at the ribbon and worked the knot loose. Eve pushed aside the cellophane.

Inside the basket, two boxes flanked the champagne bottle. Eve opened the small square box bearing a well-known chocolatier's name scripted in gold. Half-a-dozen exquisite strawberries dipped in chocolate sat nestled in tissue. Her mouth watered and her entire body tightened in response to the aroma and the memories it evoked.

Her hand wasn't quite steady as she reached for the other box. She lifted the lid, folded back the tissue paper and pulled out a red silk peignoir. The material shimmered in the fluorescent light of her office and spilled between her fingers. It was beautiful. Far better quality than the one she and Jack had ruined. She picked up a small card that had fallen to her desk.

"You look lovely in red." No signature. But then, no signature was required.

For one moment suspended in time, Eve's heart thudded. It was all exquisite.

And it infuriated her. She'd guess this wasn't the first time, nor would it be the last, that Jack sent a kiss-off gift. Dammit. She wasn't one of those women who required a present to end everything on a nice note. She'd told him she'd replace her own gown and she would.

So what was she supposed to do? Go home to her apartment, slip into the gown and think of Jack's hands and mouth touching her as the material slid against her? Bite into the tart sweetness of the strawberries and remember the way it had tasted on his lips? Open the champagne and imagine him licking it off her breasts?

She had no intention of falling for that line. She crammed everything back into the basket. Then, on second thought, pulled out the box of chocolates and popped one in her mouth. Delicious. She retied the bow around the crumpled cellophane. She picked up the card and positioned it over the shredder, but yanked it back at the last minute, shoving it into her desk drawer instead.

She desperately needed to work, but she even more desperately needed to get this package off her desk. Unfortunately, she couldn't have LaTonya send it out for her. *That* would feed the gossip mill at Hendley and Wells for weeks. No, she had to schlep it three blocks over to the Package Express store she passed every day on the way in to the office and then again on her way home.

Oh, well, she could use the exercise. She only hoped Jack had saved his receipts.

11

"WHY'D YOU send it back, Eve?"

Her note, *"Thanks, but no thanks,"* hadn't offered much explanation. When he'd been unable to dismiss her and her terse note from his mind, to the point that he couldn't concentrate on work, he'd decided to call. And it wasn't just a reason to hear her voice...although that was part of it too.

"Hello to you too, Jack." Ah, there it was. That voice, faintly amused with a dry note, knotted his gut.

"I'm doing fine," she continued. "And you?"

She was always so damned poised.

"Never better. The weather's lovely and we expect more of the same tomorrow. Now we can move on to why you returned the package," Jack said.

"I told you I'd buy myself another gown."

"But can't you accept one from me?"

"I'm not a loose end to be tied up," she said.

"Meaning?"

"Meaning it wasn't necessary for you to feel that you had to send me those things."

"I wanted to send them to you."

"And I wanted to send them back."

"What I want to understand is why." Usually women weren't a mystery to Jack. But Eve was a different matter altogether. At times, he seemed to know what was going through her head. Other times, like now, he didn't have a clue. Jack had spent some time delving into the human psyche and he knew he belonged to the less complicated of the human species.

Maybe he'd sent the wrong size—that tended to make women crazy, especially if something was too tight. Too big was a cause célèbre, but too small, watch out. "Was the gown too tight?"

"No. It wasn't too tight," she snapped. "It was too personal."

Images of the two of them in very intimate positions filtered through his mind. He could lick chocolate and strawberries off her breasts, but he couldn't replace a nightgown? "I didn't mean to overstep any boundaries. I thought we'd been fairly personal together."

"That was then. This is now."

"I think you don't want to get personal because you're afraid of me."

Her very unladylike, albeit expressive, snort came across the line loud and clear. "You're so full of... yourself. It must wear you out hauling around such a massive ego."

She paused slightly for a breath. It seemed she wasn't so poised now.

"I've got my own theory and it's a lot closer to the truth. You just can't stand it that I'm not pining for you. What am I, Jack, the one that got away? Do you want to know that you do it for me? That I hear your voice and it makes me hot."

As a matter of fact, he did want to know that. Good

news, that he affected her the same way she affected him. And despite her scathing tone, her blunt words still managed to turn him on. He felt immeasurably better. "That's a nice start. I'm pretty much in the same state."

"It's called lust," she said with derision.

"I don't have a problem with lust. It's a normal, healthy state." And he was knee-deep in it. "I can't stop thinking about you, Eve. Wanting you. Is it that way for you as well?"

"I just told you it was." Her husky tone softened, imbuing the words with sensuality.

Hearing her voice was no longer enough. "Eve, do you have video on your computer?"

"Yes. Why?"

"I want to see you. If I call, will you answer?"

"I'm not taking any clothes off," she said.

Jack laughed. "Eve, I'm not nearly as uninhibited as you seem to think I am. Getting naked on VCT is right up there with photocopying body parts in the mail room—a bad idea. I like my job. I'm looking for a promotion, not unemployment."

She laughed. "Okay. Call me. I'm equally repressed."

"I wouldn't go as far as repressed." That was one of the things he liked about Eve. She thought he was funny. Few people did. Or maybe he was only funny around her. "Give me your number." He punched in the numbers as she relayed them. Two rings and she appeared on his screen.

"Hi." Jack suddenly found himself as tongue-tied

as a teenager on prom night. "You look great." So much for originality. And it was an understatement. She looked wonderful in her red suit. Red did things for her. To be more exact, red on her did things for him. "I think I'm very sorry I agreed to the idea of keeping our clothes on." He made what he hoped was a suitably pathetic face.

She laughed at the screen and took off a pair of glasses. "How about the glasses?"

"Hmm. I rather like the glasses. Are you sure I can't talk you into taking something else off?" he teased, feeling inordinately carefree simply because he'd coaxed a smile from her.

She laughed, shaking her head, "Well, it doesn't hurt to ask," she teased.

They slipped into an easy, nonconfrontational, non-sexual conversation about work.

A knock sounded on Jack's door. "Hold on a minute," he said to Eve.

"Do I need to let you go?"

"No." He didn't want her to disappear. "Give me just a minute." He called out, "Come in."

Neville popped into his office. "Just wanted to let you know I'm heading home. Do you need anything before I'm out of here?"

Good. Nice and brief. No need to announce he was video-camming with Eve. "No. I'm fine. Thanks, Nev. Have a good evening."

Neville, however, planted his hands on the back of Jack's guest chair, facing him across the desk. "I did just hear a delicious bit of gossip...." He paused.

"From Hendley and Wells NYC." He added another pause for full dramatic effect. "It seems her Evilness swiped the Sherwood account from The Dean Group."

"Impressive," Jack said, as much for Eve's benefit as Nev's. The Dean Group held a formidable reputation in advertising. "That's quite a coup for H and W and for Eve."

Jack almost let Neville know that he wasn't technically alone, but decided against it. He was almost scot-free. Surely Nev would leave now.

"She's good, Jack. She makes me nervous."

On-screen, Eve's face blossomed in a smug grin. Jack shook his head slightly at her, encouraging her to keep her mouth shut.

She didn't. "Hi, Nervous Neville. This is her Evilness here and I'll take that as a compliment."

Neville jumped nearly a foot off the ground and glanced around wildly. "Where is she?"

Resigned, Jack shook his head and gestured toward his computer. "We were video-conferencing."

Sudden quiet filled the room.

Eve laughed, breaking the silence. "I'm not Medusa. I promise you won't turn to stone if you step forward and introduce yourself."

Nev cast a censuring look at Jack and then moved around the desk. Jack rolled his chair out of camera range. "We've got to stop meeting like this," Nev said with a tight smile as he stepped in front of the camera. "I'm Neville Hogan."

Eve introduced herself.

Neville knew when to suck up. "Congratulations. I heard you were brilliant today."

"I started that rumor." She laughed at Nev's start of surprise. "And thank you. I was lucky it went so well."

Jack and Nev both knew some days you were on and some days you weren't. The "on" days were sweet. But luck without talent didn't take you far.

"That's not what the office grapevine is saying."

"Why thank you, Nervous Nev."

Nev and Eve chatted for another few moments and seemed inclined to keep going until Jack, not so subtly, interrupted. "So, you're on your way home, Nev."

"So, I am, Jack," he mocked, and turned back to the monitor. "Does this mean I can't call you Evil One or Your Evilness now that I've met you?"

"I hope not. I rather like it."

Jack, who'd never had a possessive bone in his body, found that he was jealous of the camaraderie between Eve and his unswervingly gay assistant. He wanted her to reserve all of her clever barbs solely for himself.

Gay men weren't supposed to simper over heterosexual women unless they were Madonna or Bette Midler. But Nev had infatuation written all over his face. And Jack ought to know. That's exactly how he felt.

There, he'd admitted it. He'd come clean. He was infatuated with Eve. And perhaps there was some truth in her earlier assertion that it was her very disinterest that challenged him. But he was also drawn by the fact that Eve wasn't impressed with his money or position. She didn't even seem to like him most of the time.

His last bout of infatuation had been—it was so cliché he cringed—his nanny prior to boarding school. So, perhaps he was overdue. And this infatuation, like the previous one, would die a natural death. Eve rocked his world and turned him inside out, but there was also a sense of rightness when he was with her. In that moment, he decided she was his, whether she wanted to be or not. At least, until he decided otherwise.

"Take good care of your broom," Nev added, smirking at Eve.

"I'll do my best. Take care, Neville."

God, he was going to be sick. Nev finally dragged himself away from the monitor and to the office door, where he paused and said to Jack, "I'll check in with you later."

"Sure." He fully planned to set Nev straight. Well, not straight, but as to how things stood between him and Eve.

The door closed behind Nev, and Jack rolled his chair back into video range.

"After our first phone conversation, I never thought I'd be saying this, but Neville's actually rather charming."

White-hot jealousy knifed through him. "He's gay."

Eve looked at him as if he'd lost his mind. "So I gathered."

Maybe he *had* lost his mind, because suddenly simply seeing and hearing Eve wasn't enough. He needed to breathe in her scent, test the texture of her skin against his fingertips, and taste the sweetness of her mouth. Jack, the king of calculated moves, made a spontaneous suggestion. "What would you say if I told you I'd like to come to New York this weekend? One more side trip, just for the hell of it?"

For what seemed like an inordinate amount of time Eve took excessive interest in reshaping a paper clip. Jack's insides knotted. He'd never been turned down before, but then again, Eve was unpredictable and this might be another one of his "firsts" with her.

Then she looked up and the expression in her beautiful eyes took his breath away.

"I'd say what time are you getting in?"

"OKAY, WHAT GIVES?" Andrea asked from her sprawl in the guest chair opposite Eve's desk.

"What?"

"That's the third paper clip you've mutilated since I sat down."

Paper clips tended to suffer whenever Eve was in a funk. And she was definitely in a conundrum over Jack. "Jack's coming in on Friday."

"Let me take a wild guess. This isn't to sort out laptops."

"No. No more laptop sorting."

"I would ask why he's coming, but it's fairly obvious."

Eve had been in a state of semiarousal ever since they'd decided he'd come. "Is it?"

"My guess is he's flying in for a little follow-up fling to the original fling."

"I don't get it. It's not as if all the women just evaporated from the West Coast. San Francisco alone boasts over thirteen thousand women between the ages of twenty and thirty-four."

Andrea's recently waxed brows hiked upward.

Eve shrugged. "I know my demographics. It's part of my job." And she'd done a thirty-second web search, pathetic creature that she'd become. "Anyway, there are plenty of women there."

"Well, I'd say it's obvious—none of them are you."

"Or is it because none of them are his chief rival?"

"There is that, but I don't see the big deal unless you happen to talk in your sleep."

Eve sacrificed another paper clip and dropped it on the growing pile littering her desk. "I don't know. When he first mentioned coming, I was ready for him to be here. But I've had time to think about it, and I'm not so sure it's a good idea."

"Relax. Enjoy. It's a weekend, not a lifetime."

"My mother always said you should never date a man you wouldn't consider marrying."

"Yeah but who's looking to get married? Anyway, what's wrong with him?"

"Arrogant, wealthy, charming, too handsome for his own good, used to getting his way."

"Well, you can hardly fault him for the wealth, charm and looks. Money's not a crime unless you commit one to get it. The charm and the looks, well, honey, you're either born with them or you aren't. And as to getting his way, more power to him if he's figured out how to make that happen. About the only thing you can take exception to is the arrogance, and that just sounds as if it comes with the territory."

"You don't understand. He's—"

"Vulgar and disgusting?" Andrea suggested.

"No."

"A sexist pig?"

He'd been somewhat indignant over Bill Bradley's attitude. "Nothing like that."

"Then he's one of those guys constantly on the make, like Perry."

"No. He's very attentive."

"He's into deviant sex then? Did he want you to put him in a diaper, tie him up and then spank him while you were wearing a French maid costume?"

For a virgin, Andrea was certainly well-versed in sexual deviation. A little hollandaise sauce and champagne didn't even register when compared to Andrea's scenario. "I think you're mixing your fetishes there. But no, he's not into any of those things, that I'm aware of."

"Then chill out and have fun."

Andrea watched as Eve mutilated another paper clip. "Look, you either want him to come or you don't," she said. "If you don't, call him up and tell him you've changed your mind. But the way I see it, he's gorgeous, a decent guy, and it's one weekend. I say go for it."

So Eve could cancel and look like a weenie or go through with it and spend an entire weekend with charming, handsome Jack who wanted her job.

Was there really a choice?

12

EVE TOOK a final look around her studio apartment, make that *minuscule* studio apartment, and shook off the lingering feelings of inadequacy. She didn't want to know what kind of place Jack could afford if he lived in Manhattan. Actually, she didn't want to know how much more money Jack made than she did simply because he sported a penis. A twenty-grand gap wouldn't surprise her. Ironically, she could win the promotion, be his boss, and he might still out-earn her.

And that was just the way it was. As Andrea had pointed out, there wasn't much point in resenting Jack for inequities he had no control over. Her buzzer went off and she glanced at the clock. Traffic must've been inordinately light coming in from LaGuardia. Either that or Jack had had the cabdriver from hell. But he was here. Now. Just downstairs. Her heart pounded, but she still wasn't sure whether she was glad he was here or not.

She pressed the button. "Come on up."

"I'm on my way." Even garbled by the speaker, his voice slid over her, leaving gooseflesh in its wake.

She licked her finger and scrubbed beneath one eye and then the other. She could live without the raccoon look. She'd already changed outfits three times.

Should she go for sexy as if dressing for a hot date, dowdy to show she wasn't into dressing up for him, or home alone which was sweatpants and total slobovia? She'd opted for something in between all three. Jeans with a sort of sexy knit top. And she still wasn't sure, but it didn't matter because...Jack was knocking on her door.

She drew a deep breath. Think cool. Act cool. Be cool.

She double-checked through the peephole. Jack. In the flesh. She took off the chains, slid back the bolt and opened the door. He stood there, unsmiling, intense, almost unsure. And suddenly Eve didn't see urbane, suave yumm-o Jack the Ripper. She saw Jack the man. And anything else she wanted didn't really matter at that point. Joy welled up from somewhere deep inside her.

"Come in." She stepped aside and closed the door behind him. She turned to face him, fully intending to inquire about his trip. Instead he took a step closer to her, let his bags slide to the floor and took her into his arms. It wasn't the first time he'd done that—dropped his bags to kiss her. She liked it, rather a lot, she decided as she wound her arms around his neck, breathing his scent.

"Eve," he said, brushing the ridges of her cheekbones with his thumbs. He slid his fingers into her hair and pulled her closer, his mouth descending on hers in a tender exploration of her lips. He raised his head enough to murmur against her mouth. "This has been the longest week of my life." And then his mouth claimed hers again with a hunger and fierceness that had her straining against him. He tasted wonderful. Felt wonderful. Smelled wonderful. This was just where she wanted to be right now.

Cool air rushed against her back as Jack pulled her shirt up, his lips abandoning hers long enough to tug her top over her head and toss it to the floor. And then they were kissing again, while he trailed his lean fingers down her sides and worked loose the snap on her jeans. Eve tugged his shirt free and pulled it off, delighting in the lean heat of his body next to hers.

Jack raised his head with a grin, more like a naughty little boy, with just a touch of arrogance. "Maybe we should find the bed."

Eve shimmied her jeans lower and stepped out of them. She turned toward the bed. "Follow me," she said over her shoulder.

Jack's glance took in her skimpy red panties and matching push-up bra. "Anywhere. You know I like you in red."

She laughed. "I know."

She slid onto the mattress. Jack hopped about on one foot, trying to get his pant leg off, and finally fell into bed beside her. "I'm not winning any coordination prizes today."

Eve laughed. That's what she loved—make that *liked* about Jack. His ability to laugh at himself and make her laugh along with him. Jack's sense of humor had been a nice surprise.

Eve worked his pants off his leg with her foot. "Then we'll just have to find you another prize."

"What did you have in mind?" He stroked his hand along the length of her back and she slid her leg between his.

"We'll come up with something." She nuzzled along his neck, delighting in the feel of his shoulder against her cheek, the taste of his skin, his unique scent.

Now that they'd dispensed with everything but their underwear, flesh pressed flesh, Eve wasn't as frantic. And Jack seemed to feel the same. Their earlier impatience gave way to something softer and more languid.

Jack cupped her jaw. In Chicago, he had been a considerate lover, but now he touched her with a tenderness that made her ache.

"Eve," he breathed her name, almost a sigh, as he brushed a gossamer kiss against her lips. She kissed him back. Eve lost track of time, lost track of everything except the pleasure of kissing and being kissed. Tender and sweet. Light and flirtatious. Slow and deep. Most men seemed to only see kissing as a prelude to sex, but her Jack seemed to recognize it as an art form. And he was a master.

Before now, everything between them had been explosive. Now Eve felt like a pot simmering to a slow boil. She was hot and wet, but her limbs felt weighted, her body drugged by his kisses. His kisses awakened a longing she'd never before experienced.

Jack, his gray eyes smoky with a latent heat, fingered the red lace of her bra, his touch caressing her skin. "The only thing I like better than you in red, is you out of red."

She smiled and flicked the front hook of her bra. Jack took over from there, smoothing aside the material. He nuzzled the soft underside of her breast and the ache inside her intensified. He paused, propping himself on one elbow, looking down at her as she reclined on the bed.

Gone was the arrogance, the surety, even the humor. It was as if he was stripped of all the trappings he wore for the world and stood before her, the essence of the man, the heart of the man. Instinctively, she knew the very private man Jack was had never revealed himself this way to anybody. No one had ever seen this man. And she, who had accused Jack of being needy, realized that he was offering himself, asking only for acceptance.

"I want you, Jack," she said. It might have been stating the obvious but they both knew it was an acknowledgment, not of the man she wanted him to be, or thought him to be, but of the man he was.

As if he'd never touched her before, he feathered his hands over her face, her breasts, down her belly to remove her panties. Her body responded to his touch, absorbing the feel of his fingers, breathing in his essence.

Neither said a word as he took off his briefs and opened a condom. Eve reached up and took it from him, smoothing it down his length, sheathing him.

And then she opened herself to him and he filled her. It was beautiful and tender. Stark and raw. A giving and taking. And as she lay in Jack's arms afterward, surrounded by his warmth, she knew she'd gone somewhere she'd never been before, someplace she might never revisit. If Jack got up and walked out of her door forever, she would never be the same. For better or worse, Jack had irrevocably marked her.

"WONG'S DOES a good take-out," Eve declared on Saturday evening, putting the carton back onto the glass bistro table tucked into the corner of her galley kitchen.

"It's good. But you haven't lived until you've tried San Francisco's Chinese food," Jack said, lazily baiting her competitive side.

"Ah, a new battlefront? New York versus San Fran Chinese?"

That was his girl. He knew she'd rise to the bait. "Has anyone ever mentioned you're terribly competitive?"

"That's definitely the pot calling the kettle black." He smirked and she knew she'd been had. She lobbed a fortune cookie at him, which he neatly caught one-handed. Jack stretched his legs out in front of him, possibly more content than he'd ever been in his life.

He opened the cellophane wrapper and broke the cookie in two. He pulled out the strip of paper and read aloud. "You will win your heart's desire, if you have the wisdom to seek it." He looked up at Eve. "There you go. Sorry sweetling, but the vice presidency's mine. The cookie just said so."

Eve quirked a brow and opened hers. "A change of

fortune is forthcoming." She nodded. "I'd say that means I'll win."

He grinned at her. "I wouldn't be too sure of that."

"I'm very sure of that," she said without a hint of doubt.

And is that because you looked at my notes? The question hovered on the tip of his tongue. He'd wagered that she hadn't, but neither one of them had ever come right out and said it. He only knew that as much as he wanted this promotion, as desperately as he wanted to prove his father's predictions of failure wrong, he hadn't looked. He shook off the lingering doubt and chose a less contentious topic.

"You look about nineteen," he said. This was yet another side of Eve. Her hair was pulled up in a careless ponytail. She wore jeans and a snug T-shirt hugged her curves. Eve grimaced. "I know. Which is why you'd never catch me near the office looking this way," she said, moving to the sink and rinsing her plate.

She turned back around and Jack grabbed her wrist, tugging her onto his lap. "A very sexy nineteen," he added playfully.

"Does that make you an old lech?"

"Definitely." He grinned, wrapping his arms around her.

She ran her fingers along his stubbled jaw. "I like the scruffy look on you."

"Scruffy?"

Her eyes sparkled with devilment. "Don't sound so put out. You wear scruffy extremely well." She shifted on his lap, moving her head to one side, studying him at close range. "How old are you, Jack?"

"I thought women never wanted to discuss age."

"I'm rolling with nineteen. What about you? And don't try telling me you're nineteen."

He liked this playful side of Eve. Actually, he liked every side of Eve he'd encountered. "Thirty-one."

"When's your birthday?"

"It's fairly recent."

She furrowed her brow. "Like how recent?"

"Yesterday." He shrugged.

"Your birthday was yesterday and you didn't think you needed to mention it?"

Jack wasn't sure if she was angry or exasperated. "It's not a big deal."

"Birthdays are important," she argued. "It's a celebration of who you are." She must've read something in his face. "It wasn't that way when you were growing up, was it?"

Jack didn't share intimate details of his life, but it seemed natural to talk to Eve. "I spent most of my birthdays alone after I went to school." He traced the delicate blue vein on the underside of her wrist with his thumb. And then without considering his words, he told her what he'd never shared with anyone else. "For the first couple of years, I'd wait all day, hoping my parents would show up or at least call."

"Your parents—" Eve stumbled, furious, but apparently wary of insulting his lineage.

"Were busy," he supplied.

"Humph," she snorted. Eve, this magnificent

woman, would be more than a match for his parents. "I wish you'd told me it was your birthday yesterday."

"I just did."

She glared at him. "I meant yesterday."

He brought the soft underside of her wrist to his lips and pressed a kiss against her warm, satin skin. "Eve, yesterday was the best birthday I've ever had." He kissed the tender spot inside her elbow and felt the quiver that arced through her. He was acutely aware of the press of her buttocks against his crotch, the soft fullness of her breast within inches of his chest, her womanly scent that was uniquely hers. "I was exactly where I wanted to be, doing what I wanted to do, with the person I wanted to be doing it with."

"Jack..." She winnowed her hands through his hair and tugged his head to her. Her breath was warm and redolent with fresh ginger.

The phone rang and Eve made no move to answer it. "The answering machine can get it."

Her lips skimmed his. A brush. A promise. A prelude.

The machine picked up with Eve's recorded voice instructing the caller to leave a message. "Hi, baby, it's just me," a woman's voice announced, obviously her mother. It was something of a mood breaker.

"Listen, your brother Bryan is in the city this weekend for a conference. His friend Tobias is also there. Dad and I thought you might like to meet him. Maybe you can join them for dinner one evening. Call him on his cell phone if you get this message, that is if you're not out of town on that job of yours."

Disdain, no, more along the line of exasperation, came through loud and clear. "Try to work it out to meet them, okay, honey? And I hope you're not sitting there and not picking up the phone." Her mother hung up and the answering machine clicked off.

"Kind of eerie the way she seems to know when I'm just not answering. Must be mother's intuition." An interesting combination of guilt, defiance and something else colored Eve's face.

Jack wouldn't know. His mother didn't seem to possess a motherly instinct one way or another. "You weren't kidding. She really doesn't think much of your job."

"You could tell, huh?"

"Loud and clear. So, it looks as if I'm throwing a kink in your dinner plans with the prospective Tobias." He tried to sound remorseful rather than pleased.

"Even if you weren't here, I wouldn't meet them for dinner. This is just this month's attempted fix-up. Every couple of months, my parents harangue my brothers into dragging out one of their friends like a consolation prize. I told you. They barely tolerate the job and they want me married off."

"How long has this been going on?"

Eve sighed. "Since my senior year in college, when they realized I intended to graduate and get a job. They're very traditional."

"They've given up on you finding your own husband so they're hunting one down for you now?" As if Eve couldn't find a man on her own. What a ridiculous notion.

"Something like that. They mean it in the kindest way possible. They simply don't understand how I can possibly be happy with just a career. And they do want me to be happy. They just don't understand how I can enjoy my current lifestyle."

"Do you?" He wanted to know everything about her.

"Yes. I have good friends. I'm healthy. I love my job and this city." She glanced around her. "My apartment could be bigger." *The closet in his condo was only marginally smaller than her walk-up.* "I could get that promotion at work." *He was trying his damnedest to see that she didn't.* "I could lose ten pounds."

"Please, no. I've so enjoyed every inch of you, I'm not sure what ten pounds I could bear to do without," he countered with a leer, curling his fingers around her hip.

She laughed and pressed a quick kiss to his mouth. "That's very gallant of you. But there's no gaping void in my life." She looked at him. "So, contrary to their opinion, I don't need a man to complete me." She laughed again, keeping it light, but her message came through loud and clear.

His leg was going numb where she was sitting on his lap, but asking her to move now seemed very poor timing on his part. "And what would your parents say about me?"

She cocked her head to one side and considered him. "I don't honestly know."

"I have a good job. My family's well-off. Most people would consider me a good catch. I actually overheard a couple of mothers call me that at a cocktail party once."

"Okay, okay, you're a dream prospect. But the telling factor is whether you want your wife and kids waiting on you when you come home every day."

"I've never really thought about it. I've been perfectly content without a wife." Just as a frame of reference, certainly nothing more, he plugged Eve into his equation. "I would want my wife to do whatever made her happy. Whatever fulfilled her."

"That's a nice pat answer."

"It's the truth. What would be the point in being married to someone who was miserable? No marriage stands a chance when one of the parties resents the other. At least that's what I've observed." And he'd spent a lifetime observing other people live.

She slid off of his lap and walked to the room's double window. "Why are you really here, Jack?" she asked with her back to him.

"Because I want to be here."

She turned to face him, leaning against the windowsill, backlit by the sun. "Okay, then why do you want to be here? What's in it for you, other than the obvious sex, which I can't believe you have to fly across the country to get. So, let me ask you again, why do you want to be here? Why would you choose to spend your birthday with me?"

"Because I find you interesting. You fascinate me. I've never met anyone quite like you before."

"Jack, there are women like me everywhere. Look around you. There are lots of career-oriented, intelligent women with chocolate fixations."

"Perhaps. But none of them are you. Now why don't you tell me why I'm here? Why did you tell me I could come for the weekend?"

"I suppose my reasons are the same as yours. You're an interesting man. And we both know the score. Once one of us wins, there's nowhere else to go with this."

Her answer should've satisfied him. But he'd never felt less satisfied in his life.

"IT WAS A NICE WEEKEND," Jack said, tucking his shaving kit into his bag.

Understatement. It'd been so great it was scary. They'd discovered they shared many common interests—especially an affinity for live theater, Szechuan dumplings, single-malt Scotch, and reading the *Times* from cover to cover—in addition to great sex. Despite the constant presence of the Bradley account and the vague distrust between them, they'd enjoyed an easy companionship.

"Except for the bathroom." Which in her tiny apartment was tinier still. Eve smiled remembering how they'd squeezed in there together—it must have been like making love in an airplane washroom.

He offered her a wicked smile. "I don't have a problem with your bathroom at all. I'll think of it fondly. By the way are you here all week?"

The steam radiator hissed on and Eve cracked the window so it wouldn't fog over. "I'm in Dallas overnight on Tuesday, but then I'm back in the city. How about you?"

"Tuesday and Wednesday in Seattle." He zipped his travel bag. "Have you ever been to San Francisco?"

"We had a meeting there last year, at the office. It's a nice city and I loved the office space." Former warehouse space now housed the sophisticated, ultra-chic Hendley and Wells West Coast office. Jack would fit right in there.

Jack left his bag on the bed and bracketed her shoulders with his hands. A sensuous shiver slid through her. "Why don't you fly out next weekend?"

Whoa. It was one thing to allow him to come here. But going to San Francisco? The idea sent her into a tailspin. "Jack, I'm on a fairly tight budget and I can't afford it."

He traced a lazy path along her collarbone with one finger. "Don't you have frequent flier miles?"

She pulled away from him. His touch muddled her thinking. "I'm going to Italy in the fall and I'm using my points for that ticket."

"Anyone special there?"

"No. My friend Andrea has relatives there." She'd almost think he was jealous if she didn't know better.

"I'll pay for your ticket to San Francisco."

"Absolutely not." That felt too much like being a

kept woman, which totally offended her independence. "And anyway, I need to work next weekend. We're presenting the following week—"

"I know. I think we've moved past the stealing idea phase."

Except she'd never know for sure whether he'd looked or not. "I suppose. You know, only one of us can win and that will change...well, everything." Whatever their relationship was or wasn't, it was running on borrowed time. "I don't think either one of us is capable of losing graciously."

Whether she liked Jack or hated him would be immaterial week after next. What was one more weekend out of a lifetime? She drew a deep breath. "You're welcome to come back to New York next week. We could each get in some time on the Bradley account if you promise not to peek."

Jack possessed a killer smile. But when he smiled with his eyes, it was devastating. He offered her one of those smiles now, obviously pleased with her invitation. "Only if you're asking me not to peek at the project. I'm not sure that I can promise not to look at anything else."

"I could look into getting tickets to an off-Broadway show for Saturday night."

"That would be excellent." His watch alarm went off. He pushed a button, silencing it. "I've got to leave for the airport," he said without moving.

Eve knew she had a way of holding herself back. She was more than a willing participant, but Jack was the one who initiated contact. It was Jack who reached for her or pulled her onto his lap or into his arms or touched her.

This time, Eve made the first move, sliding her arms around his neck and kissing him, telling him with her lips and her tongue how much she'd miss him. He kissed her back as if he were storing up a week's worth of her to take with him.

Reluctantly they pulled apart. "I've got to catch my cab or I'll miss my flight. I'll bring chocolate."

He'd brought her lovely chocolate-dipped strawberries this time. And they'd tasted even better than she'd imagined when she'd ate them off of him.

"Then by all means, I'll look forward to seeing you on Friday." She smiled, which was better than crying, which was what she actually felt like doing. Of their own will, her fingers caressed the lean line of his jaw. "Travel safe, Jack."

Jack picked up his bag. Eve stood still, undecided whether she should offer to go down to the curb with him or not. And then he was gone and it didn't matter. She went to the window and watched the sidewalk. Within a few seconds Jack appeared and hailed a cab. He was a lucky devil because, while Eve had sometimes waited as long as five minutes for a cab, one immediately pulled to the curb for Jack. He opened the back door, but turned before he got in and seemed to look straight at her, as serious as when he'd first arrived. Too late to step back, he'd already seen her watching his departure. Neither one waved but each acknowledged the other.

Jack turned around and climbed in. The yellow cab merged into traffic and he was gone.

She should be glad. She'd lived alone since college. She liked living alone. She should've felt crowded and confined, but there'd been something cozy and comforting about sharing her space with Jack. What was worse, she suddenly realized it would be far too easy to get used to having him in her life.

13

"ANOTHER WEEKEND with Evil Eve?" Nev drawled from the doorway.

Surprised, Jack looked up from his notes. "What makes you think I'm spending my weekends with Eve?" he asked, neither confirming nor denying. Nev liked to speculate.

"Come on, Jack. Did you think it had escaped my notice that you're leaving early again today, same as you did last Friday. And you have your overnight bag with you again," he said, gesturing to the bag in the corner. "You didn't call me once last weekend, so I know you weren't in here with your nose to the grind. No new chica is calling you and you very pointedly haven't mentioned a new woman. So brilliant person that I am, I've surmised that you've fallen under the Evil One's spell. In fact, I think you tumbled the Evil One while the two of you were in Chicago. And then, there's that look you get every time her name is mentioned."

Neville was too damn clever for his own good. His best bet was to downplay their...attraction? Relationship? Fling? He didn't know exactly what they had, but he'd downplay it. "Not much gets past you does it, Nev? Eve and I have been seeing one another. But we thought it best not to invite gossip, so we kept it quiet."

Nev looked like the proverbial cat who'd found a bowl of cream. "Well, not that you need my blessing or anything but...I approve."

"Your approval means a lot to me, Nev. You've been more of a family to me than the one I've got. You're a good friend." Jack felt closer to Nev than he did to either one of his siblings. And it was something he should have told Neville a long time ago.

Nev preened. "It took you long enough to figure it out. But I won't be swayed off topic by your declarations of appreciation. How do you feel about *her?*"

"She's sarcastic, temperamental, talented, smart, outspoken. Oh yeah, independent, too."

"Thanks, Jack. I figured all that out on my own. But how do you feel about her?"

"I like her."

"That's good news since you spent last weekend shacking up with her, and you're going back for seconds."

Actually, it was saying more than Neville knew. Until Jack had spent time with Eve, he hadn't realized that he didn't really like any of the women he'd slept with before. He didn't actually dislike them. He'd just been generally ambivalent.

"She's intriguing."

"But how do you *feel* about her?"

Couldn't Nev simply be satisfied with an admission of attraction? Jack was more than satisfied not to dig any deeper. "How the hell am I supposed to know? I don't do that 'I feel...' stuff."

"Well, for God's sake, don't look so disgusted. It's not as if your *thing* is going to fall off if you confess to having a feeling." Nev heaved a sigh and rolled his eyes as if seeking forbearance. "Okay. Leave it to 'moi' to walk you through this. It's not that hard. How do you feel when you leave Eve each weekend?" Neville enunciated each word of the question slowly, as if he were dealing with a dimwit.

Jack was at a total loss. He generally didn't discuss feelings. "How do I feel when I leave?"

"Jack. It's not a trick question. I'm assuming you enjoyed your weekend or you wouldn't be going back. But when you got back home, were you relieved to be back in your own space? Happy to have some time alone in your fabulous condo with the stunning view of the Golden Gate?" Nev had never hidden the fact that he had major condo envy.

That he could answer. "No. It's odd. With every other woman I've dated, I always felt like they were crowding me. I needed my space. When I'm with Eve, there's Eve, but I still have my space. And when I'm not with her, I miss her."

That was an abysmal understatement. When they were apart, she was like a hunger that gnawed at him. He missed the taste of her, the feel of her wrapped around him. The sex was great, but he also liked sitting in her apartment on Sunday morning with fresh bagels and lattes, listening to lazy jazz with the sounds of the city in the background, swapping off sections of the *Times*, discussing articles of interest.

"So, what are you going to do about it?"

"I'm not going to *do* anything other than show up for one last weekend. From day one this has been short-term, Nev. It's pretty amazing that it's gone on this long. And quite frankly, I believe in quitting while we're still ahead in the game."

"That's stupid. You're being a chicken shit, by the way."

"What? I should wait for her to tell me it's over? I don't think so."

"So, you're fine with walking away?"

Damn Nev and his questions. "Pretty much."

"So it wouldn't be a problem to think of her with someone else?"

"Possessiveness doesn't mean anything except an unwillingess to share."

"Has it every occurred to you that you might be in love with her?"

No. It was impossible. Only fools... "I don't believe in love."

Neville laughed.

"What's so funny?"

"You." He shook his head as if Jack's naivety overwhelmed him. "It doesn't matter whether you believe in love or not. My cousin Adolpho—" Neville had a big family with a bunch of weird names "—didn't believe in ghosts. So Adolpho moved right into a regular haunted mansion. Those ghosts didn't give a fig whether or not he believed in them. They spooked his ass off. Trust me, no one in the family would go for a visit and it made a believer out of him."

"Let's suppose for the sake of argument that I'm head over heels," Jack said, ignoring Nev's smirk. "I don't see that it makes much difference. She's the singular most self-sufficient woman I've ever met."

"Correct me if I'm wrong, but I believe that's one of her attractions for you."

"You know, I probably should have spent some of my unlimited funds on a good therapist years ago. I'm so screwed up, her indifferent tolerance of me is one of her attractions. Next I'll want her to tie me up and call me trash," said Jack.

"Well, much as it probably would go against the grain for her, she would probably do it. I think beneath it all, she cares for you."

"Why in the world would you think that?" It was ridiculous how important Nev's answer was to him.

"How many women have been willing to date you because you looked good and your family was loaded?" Nev didn't wait for an answer. "I think you're so riddled with insecurity because Eve is all about the real man beneath the pretty exterior and the big bucks."

"So, you're suggesting I profess undying love?"

Nev arched his brows. "Only if that's how you feel."

He'd always been indifferent about his relationships, and that indifference always had him walking away first. But he didn't feel indifferent in the least now. How would it feel if Eve turned him down? "And what if she..."

"Rejects you?"

"Thank you, Neville, for spelling that out. It's even warmer, fuzzier, put into words. Now exactly why would I want to put myself in that position?"

"Consider this practice and you tell me."

Jack looked at Neville, feeling extremely foolish. As a matter of course, he didn't do foolish.

"Come on. Say it."

There was the old adage that it was darkest before the dawn. This should certainly qualify. He was about to profess his love for Eve aloud to his gay assistant in San Francisco. It was abjectly pathetic. Even more so, because he was going through with it.

"I love Eve." The words felt awkward against his tongue. He hadn't told anyone he loved them since before he'd been shipped off to boarding school. That was a damn long time. He'd deemed it lust at first sight. How arrogant on his part. He'd been smitten from the first moment she'd pulled off that ridiculous swim cap. "I love her."

Neville clapped his hands together. "Oh, Jack."

Had a choir broken into song, he wouldn't have been surprised, the whole thing felt so surreal. "That wasn't so hard," he said. It had actually been rather cathartic. She'd called him needy and, in retrospect, he could see that he had been. But now he didn't need to take as much as he needed to give.

"Good. But that was only practice. Now you have to tell Eve."

Oh. Yeah.

JACK SPOONED his body around hers, even as orgasmic aftershocks rolled through her. Who would have ever guessed that Jack "The Ripper" LaRoux was a cuddler? The warmth of his chest and thighs and legs molded to her. He curled his arm across her midriff, the back of his hand nestled beneath the underside of her breast. His harsh breathing stirred against the back of her neck and shoulder.

It was nice—even on the floor. A six-foot expanse of floor stretched between them and the bed. She'd thought the incredible chemistry between them would've started showing signs of diminishing but, if anything, it had intensified. They hadn't even made it as far as the bed.

It was definitely time to call it quits with Jack, before she got any more addicted to him than she already was.

He pressed a light kiss against her shoulder and her stomach fluttered. Later. She'd tell him later that this was their last weekend. He brushed his hand across her belly and she quivered. Yes, much, much later. But for now, she gave herself up to the pleasure of lying on the floor naked with Jack.

She rolled onto her back, the wood floor cool against her buttocks and back. She stretched, laughing quietly. "I think I bruised my...knees." The last word came out faintly. The stark tenderness in his eyes, on his face, shook her. "Jack?"

"I love you." Those three simple words shifted her world on its axis.

She closed her eyes and lay very still. "Please don't say that. I don't expect to hear it. I don't want to hear it."

"Eve, look at me." Slowly she opened her eyes. Jack was propped on one elbow, his eyes dark, intense. "Surely you don't think I make a habit of this."

No. Deep inside she knew he didn't. "You surprised me." And then some. She'd been mentally rehearsing goodbyes and he'd been rehearsing a declaration of love?

"It kind of surprised me, as well." A smile hovered about his mouth.

She rolled to her feet, grabbing the first piece of clothing within reach. She pulled on Jack's shirt, which hung to mid-thigh. "You can't have thought this through."

Jack stood, seemingly content to remain naked. "You know, when you have a topic you want to avoid, you make unflattering personal comments. Yes, I have thought it through."

"We live on opposite sides of the country."

He shrugged. "Logistics. One of us could move. In fact, I'll have to move to take on the new position." He said it so matter-of-factly, so sure of himself, that Eve was more convinced than ever that he'd rifled through her notes.

This was the man who'd deemed love a myth, two short weeks ago? The part of her that couldn't trust him, also couldn't trust his change of heart, much as she was tempted to. "What about the man who doesn't believe in love?"

"Love doesn't care whether you believe in it or not."

Eve couldn't have been more surprised had a group of Mongol Sherpas, complete with laden yak, trekked through her apartment. "Did you take some kind of drugs or something? This is so not you."

Impatience, exasperation, arrogance flashed across his face and he looked more like the Jack she knew and...liked...and didn't trust. "I assume you're being facetious. I'm trying to be sensitive and humble and apparently, I'm botching it."

Eve didn't trust him. Couldn't trust him. Jack wasn't the kind of man she'd envisioned building a future with. He was too...well, everything. Too sexy. Too handsome. Too arrogant. Too competitive. Too compelling. Jack was simply too Jack. How did you live with a man like Jack and not lose sight of yourself in the process? And perhaps underlying everything was the fear that if she truly gave her heart to Jack, he would lose interest. Jack wasn't a happily-ever-after kind of guy. And maybe, beneath it all, she didn't trust herself not to, once again, fall short of the mark.

"I don't think so, Jack. We have a good time together, but I just don't see it working out. Perhaps after this weekend, we should aim for a good, clean break."

"You still haven't given me a good reason why." On most other men, it would've sounded like whining.

But not Jack. It just sounded as if he demanded an explanation he could buy into.

"Jack, we have great sex together. You can't call that love. This *thing* between us will wear itself out sooner or later." She presented the argument as much for her sake as his. She couldn't have been foolish enough to fall in love with Jack.

Jack shook his head. "I think I was in love with you, the idea of you, before I ever met you. I'd studied your work and I admired and respected you. And then I met you and the reality of you was even better than the woman I'd imagined. I've never felt this way about anyone before."

His words tore at her. She sank to the edge of her bed. "I'm sure there'll be others—"

"I'm sure there won't be. It's as if I was locked inside myself until I met you. I've lived my whole life watching, observing, but never really living. You're the key that unlocked me."

She clasped her hands in her lap to keep them from shaking. That was simply the most beautiful thing she'd ever heard. And if she allowed herself to believe it and found out he'd used her, twisted their relationship to give him the advantage with the account, she'd never forgive either one of them. "That's lovely. And flattering. But, I don't want that kind of responsibility. I don't want to think that if I make a mistake or say something wrong, that I'm going to shut you down."

"It's a two-way street. Whether you want it or not, you do need someone to love you. Someone to celebrate your wins, mourn your losses and cover the times in between." He nuzzled the sensitive area of her neck between her ear and shoulder. "Bagels in bed, chocolate and champagne breakfasts."

"And would you celebrate my wins, Jack? I'm not sure that your ego will allow it and I won't sacrifice something I love, my job, my talent, for someone's ego. I'm sorry. Truly I am. And I'm flattered. Immensely. But I don't love you."

"I don't believe you."

"You don't have to. I believe me and that's what counts."

"I love you. Not just for today or tomorrow. I can be patient."

Eve's nerves were wrecked and she reached for one of the chocolates Jack had brought her a week ago.

"You might find that together we're better than chocolate," he teased in an obvious attempt to lighten things up.

"Nothing is better than chocolate."

JACK SETTLED BACK into the first-class seat. Considering the start they'd gotten off to, the weekend with Eve had turned out well. Really, in retrospect, he hadn't expected her to fall into his arms with a reciprocal declaration. He'd gone into it knowing he had an uphill battle to convince her of the rightness of the two of them. He knew he was going to have to earn Eve's trust. Once he had the vice presidency and had moved to Manhattan, she'd see that things could work out between them.

The idea ran through his mind that perhaps she was

playing him, keeping him off-kilter to throw his presentation. But then again, she was the one who was running away, not him. Maybe she was just intensely cunning and it was a ruse. He'd be damn glad to get this presentation over with and have Bill Bradley make a decision. Thursday he'd be back on a plane. This time to make his pitch to Bradley. Once they made their presentations, surely Eve would realize he hadn't looked at her notes, that she could trust him. And then they'd get on with building a relationship.

"I BELIEVE YOU AND Jack have met," Kirk Hendley said with a sharp smile that said he enjoyed the tension running between Eve and Jack. Andrea might've been on to something. Kirk was rather sadistic, orchestrating his own corporate cockfight. Only he didn't know that privately Eve and Jack had turned this into a to-the-death match. Kirk didn't usually attend presentations, but apparently he wasn't willing to miss his two best talents going head-to-head.

"Jack, good to see you again," Eve said, and offered her hand.

"Eve," he acknowledged, giving her a brief but firm shake. His touch coursed through her. One would think that after three weeks of those long, lean fingers exploring her intimately, she would've become immune to his touch. No. A simple, professional handshake left her tingling in very unprofessional places.

"You guys are gonna knock Bradley's socks off. I think this is the best campaign either one of you has ever turned out." Kirk had seen both of their proposals, although they still hadn't seen each other's. Nor had they discussed it with one another.

"I think Mr. Bradley will be pleased," Jack said.

Eve reserved comment as they crossed the lobby to the elevator bank.

Kirk discussed the West Coast office with Jack during the ride up. She'd had Kirk's undivided attention on the plane trip from New York to Chicago and throughout the cab ride from O'Hare. She zoned now, mentally running through the salient points of her presentation.

They reached Bradley's office and Jack and Eve waited in the vestibule while Kirk approached the receptionist—their first, and probably only, opportunity for a personal, private conversation.

Eve turned to Jack. "Good luck," she said. She meant it. She wanted him to feel he'd done his absolute best when she won.

"Same to you. I know you've worked hard, but so has my whole team." Eve had the distinct impression he was apologizing ahead of time for winning.

She tamped down her uncertainty. "Yes, my team has worked very hard, too." She offered her most professional, impersonal smile.

Jack, coolly arrogant, returned the smile and Eve reminded herself there was another Jack underneath, a man she'd rolled around naked with not so long ago. Only one of them could win today and she sincerely hoped it was whoever had turned out the best product.

"I can't wait to see yours as well." She had her back

to the office and dropped him a wink. After a startled moment, he laughed, diffusing the tension between them.

The moment passed as Bradley and Kirk Hendley approached. The same calm, with a couple of butterflies to keep her on her toes, settled over her that she always experienced prior to this kind of meeting.

"May the best...person win," Jack murmured as they were sucked into the group.

This was where it had all begun and this is where it would end. Who wound up on top, was, after all, what it was all about, wasn't it?

"BRILLIANT," Kirk commended them both, waiting until they were in the cab bound for the airport to throw out the pronouncement.

Eve was near euphoric. It wasn't just because it was over and had gone well. The best part was that Jack's presentation had been so far removed from her own. There was absolutely no way Jack had looked at her notes. Win or lose, she felt as if a tremendous weight had been lifted from her shoulders.

Much as it galled her, she had to seriously contend with losing. Self-confidence could only take you so far. And it was one thing when you knew your product was superior to another. Hers wasn't. It had been a very tight presentation, but it wasn't necessarily better. Her team's angle had a more hip, "with it" edge, playing to the female market, which is what she thought Bradley needed, not only to recoup lost market share but also to catapult him into the lead. Jack had offered a more conservative/traditional approach, innovative but not designed to pull Bradley out of his comfort zone. It simply came down to Bradley's preference.

"Very nice job," she said to Jack.

"You too. That approach was inspired," Jack said, a chill underlying his tone and the look in his eyes.

Eve had to choose her words carefully in front of Kirk, but she wanted to let Jack know she realized he hadn't looked at her notes when he had the opportunity. They'd overcome the trust issue. "And we each gave him something very different. I was a bit concerned our projects might be too similar."

"Really? I hope you didn't lose any sleep over it." Despite his affable, light tone, his eyes were glacial.

Jack was acting strange. If she didn't know better, she'd think he was furious. But then presenting could do strange things to people and she'd never observed Jack in this capacity before. Personally, she was exhausted. Emotional denouement.

First there was the whole dog-and-pony show. She'd had to follow Jack which was a bit nerve-racking, then lunch with Jack, Kirk, Bradley and his in-house advertising/promotions manager.

"There's a very real possibility Bradley might want to combine the campaigns. They were so distinctly different and each had such distinguishing strengths," Kirk said.

The "L" rumbled past on its overhead track, rendering conversation impossible. She'd take New York's subway any day. When the train had passed, Kirk resumed his musing.

"I watched him and there was definite interest in distinctly different elements of your proposals." He stroked his rather narrow chin consideringly. "Yeah, that's a possibility. I'm sure you two could work together." Kirk bore a striking resemblance to Andrea's ferret when he grinned. "We wouldn't be the first firm to have co vice presidents."

That possibility hadn't occurred to her. Could she and Jack work together as partners? And what would that do to the salary? She couldn't fathom that H and W would willingly double what they'd budgeted for the position. She'd have to manage Jack's arrogance to make sure he didn't try to railroad her, but from the time they'd spent together, she knew there was almost a synergy between the two of them that could turn out some awesome products. She shrugged, unwilling to openly speculate. Jack simply smiled. It wasn't a particularly nice smile.

Kirk, not finding any conversational takers, lapsed into his own silence. Kirk understood, as Eve knew from past presentations, just how draining it could be for the account execs.

The cab pulled curbside at the airport and Jack, Kirk and Eve climbed out. "Okay, I'm off to Tulsa. Good job today." Kirk hurried off, obviously dismissing them and mentally moving on to his dinner meeting with a potential client.

"I believe the Tulsa project will go to you if we get it," Eve said to Jack.

Jack turned and looked at her with such contempt she nearly recoiled. "Very nice job, Eve. It was a brilliant performance on all counts."

This man was a stranger. "What's wrong with you, Jack? My presentation wasn't any better than yours."

"Oh, sweetling, I'm not talking about today. I'm talking about your performance for the last two weeks. God, how did you keep from laughing yourself silly when I professed eternal love...well, that reflects true talent." His look of admiration was deliberately insulting. "You make Machiavelli look like a choirboy."

Eve felt as if she'd been slapped. "If you're going to toss out accusations, you at least owe me an explanation."

"You can dispense with the outrage act. It served you well before, but we've moved beyond that now."

Eve was vaguely aware of the people moving around them, past them, but for the most part, she felt as if she'd stepped in a hole and was free-falling. "If you want to have a dialogue, then you have to tell me what you're talking about, because I'm clueless."

"Okay. Apparently you'll derive some sort of pleasure from hearing me say it. I had two ideas outlined in my notes. Two columns. Side by side. I ditched one idea, drew a line threw it, because I didn't think I could convince Bradley to go there. And voilà, I hear my discarded idea parroted back today in your presentation. You, at least, made some alterations in approach and execution."

Eve wasn't sure her legs would support her. Jack

thought she'd stolen his idea. Jack thought she was a cheat. Stunned, she remained speechless. Which was just as well because apparently Jack wasn't through.

"Oh, honey, you really knew how to play that outraged integrity schtick. I'm sure you got a little more than you bargained for when I threw myself prostrate at your feet. Small wonder you were countering every argument I presented. You told me from the beginning nothing was more important to you than winning this promotion, and still, I underestimated you."

"Jack, I understand how it must look—"

"You are clever."

She ignored his scathing interruption, trying to remain calm, trying to fix this. "I know how it looks, but I did not read your notes. I pulled them out, realized they weren't mine and put them away. I thought about it, I admit. All the way back to New York, I thought about how much I wanted the promotion and the advantage I could gain. But I couldn't do it. I *didn't* do it."

"So, I'm supposed to believe you just came up with the same idea? I won't be made a fool twice, Eve."

Mentally she scrambled for a way to convince him. "I can tell you where the idea came from. The night we met, before we went into the restaurant, we discussed high-maintenance women. I was mentally running through my head all the ways I wasn't a high-maintenance woman. Later, when we were in bed, after we'd made love, I was in that semi-sleep stage when ideas seem to run through my stream of consciousness. I started thinking about other women who weren't high maintenance. Independent. One thought led to another. Women who'd mow their own lawn. Plow their own field. It sounds sort of crazy, but you're creative. You know how one small kernel of conversation can grow into an idea."

Jack stood unmoving, a closed expression on his face. "That's a very nice story, Eve. I'm sure you've had it prepared for some time now. You've thoroughly covered your bases. Do you have any other fictional accounts you'd like to offer up?"

Eve knew when to cut her losses. There'd be no convincing Jack today, and quite frankly, now that the anesthesia of surprise was wearing off, she was beginning to get royally pissed that he thought her incapable of coming up with a winning campaign of her own. He wanted to impugn her integrity, her professionalism? "No fiction. Here's a slice of reality for you. Shove it up your ass, Jack."

"YOU LOOK LIKE HELL."

"Thank you. And good morning to you too, Nev." Jack strode past Neville's desk and into his office, pointedly closing the door.

The door opened before he even made it to his chair.

"You could've at least answered your cell phone. I've only been waiting sixteen hours to hear how the presentation went."

"I didn't want to talk to anyone."

"That's fine. But you have a conference call with Eve and Kirk Hendley in less than five minutes. Apparently Bill Bradley made the world's quickest decision. Kirk called him back from Tulsa this morning."

Jack didn't ask how Nev knew all of this. Nev had his sources. His gut clenched. "Do you know which pitch he chose?"

"That I don't know. No one knows but Kirk and he's not talking until he has both you and Eve on the line."

He was about to get the most important news of his career and he was still so angry about Eve, he almost didn't give a damn. "Fine."

Neville closed the office door and plopped down in the chair facing Jack. "You give a career-making presentation, don't answer your cell phone, skip half a day of work and finally show up in a bitch of a mood. We've got three minutes. Talk to me, Jack."

Jack still felt on the verge of exploding. Even extra laps this morning hadn't managed to dispel his anger. Maybe talking to Nev would help. Better to vent before he got on the phone with his conniving counterpart and Kirk Hendley. "She stole my idea, Nev. Stole it and ran with it."

"Are you sure, Jack?" For once, Nev lost his hyperbole.

Jack yanked his notes out of his briefcase and threw the papers on the desk. "Right there." He jabbed his finger at the right-hand column, which had been penciled through. "That was Eve's presentation."

"Are you sure, Jack?"

What, was Nev stuck on one phrase? "I was there. Yes, I'm sure that's what she presented."

"But are you sure she got the idea from you?"

"I don't believe in coincidence." He checked his watch. "Get Kirk and Eve on the line. I don't want to be late for this call."

"One thing to bear in mind, Jack—" Nev paused at the door. "Great minds tend to think alike," he said before he slipped out of the room.

"WE HAVE A BIT of a grapevine here at H and W, so I'm sure you two have already heard that Bradley's made a decision." Kirk's disembodied voice came clearly through the phone line.

"Yes," Eve said. She heard Jack's affirmative on his

end. Despite her exhaustion yesterday, Eve hadn't slept at all. Jack's accusations had kept her up most of the night.

"Well, you both did a superb job, as we discussed yesterday, and I really thought we might wind up with both of you moving into the position," Kirk droned on.

Eve bit her lip to keep from screaming at him to hurry up and tell them. She, who never suffered from nerves, was a wreck. She was sure it was only her overactive imagination fueled by a lack of sleep, but she could swear she felt Jack's nervous tension on the other end of the line as well.

"Bradley was very pleased with both presentations, very pleased indeed. And he looks forward to working with us on the rollout. So, I'm sure you're both anxious to know...." *Hurry up.* "Our new marketing vice president is Eve. Congratulations, Eve."

Yes, she'd done it. They'd done it. She was now the vice president of one of the most upwardly mobile, small ad agencies in the country. "I'm very pleased for my team." Her calm, steady voice didn't betray her racing heart.

"Congratulations, Eve." Jack did a good job of sounding sincere for Kirk's benefit.

"Thank you."

Kirk laughed. "I think Bradley felt a little foolish that they'd ignored the female market for so long."

"I think it will turn their business around," Eve said.

"So does Bradley and this will be a big boost for our

business too. Jack, he wanted to incorporate some of your elements as well, if you'd be willing to work with Eve on the rollout."

"Of course. Whatever I can do to help. I'll be glad to give her any ideas she needs," Jack said.

His hidden barb stung. "Thank you, Jack. It's good to know you're there if I need you." She felt sure he'd receive her underlying sarcasm. This should be one of the happiest moments of her life. She was angry with herself that Jack held the power to diminish it.

"I've got a plane to catch. We'll firm up the details when I'm back in the office tomorrow, Eve," Kirk said.

Everyone said goodbye and hung up. As soon as she hung up the line, her team rushed her door.

"We won," she yelled, pasting on a smile. "We did it."

Everyone hurried into the room, cheering, hugging and high-fiving. Within minutes, it had been decided that celebratory drinks were called for. Eve, caught up in crowd, went along with the group to celebrate the biggest achievement of her career.

Two dogs. One bone. And she'd won. She'd gotten what she asked for. But what had she lost along the way?

HE'D LOST. The most important campaign of his career and he'd blown it. He'd opted for the safe approach, Eve had climbed out on a limb, and she'd won.

Disappointment ripped at his gut. He could nix the idea of the triumphant return of the prodigal son.

Neville knocked and entered without waiting for

Jack to invite him in. He looked at Jack. "Her Evilness won, didn't she?"

Jack ran his hand over his forehead. "I'm sorry, Nev." Not only had he let himself down, he'd let his team down.

Nev shrugged and sank into the chair. "No apology necessary. We all know that in this business you win some and you lose some. We were due a loss."

Didn't Nev even care? "Obviously I'm confused. I thought you wanted this as much as I did. It was a helluva time to come in with a loss."

"My Aunt Berta—" Neville had an aunt named Berta? "—always said sometimes losing is more important than winning."

"It sounds to me as if Aunt Berta was full of...platitudes."

"Think what you like. According to her, there were equally important lessons to be learned whether you won or lost. What'd you lose today, Jack? Really lose? A pay raise you didn't need? A chance to thumb your nose at your wretched father? Self-esteem? Did you really need this to validate how outrageously good you are at your job? Those are just things, Jack, and not really very important things."

"In a frightening way, you're making sense." Jack leaned forward, propping his arms on his desk, taking Nev's words to heart.

"Jack, forget intellect. I'm going to ask you a question and I want the gut response that comes from your heart, not your head. Do you really think Eve stole your idea?"

"It was right there in black and white."

Nev wagged an admonishing finger. "I don't want to hear about black and white. Isn't that why you were so angry, so hurt, because you fell in love with a woman of integrity and then she let you down? Remember what I told you yesterday? Great minds think alike. I think you and Her Evilness are two peas in a pod beneath it all. Small wonder you'd come up with similar ideas."

His head had ruled his life for so long, it was difficult to listen to his heart, to trust in his heart. But he knew he was at an important juncture in his life. He could go back to his detached existence, observing the world, watching life literally pass him by. Or he could listen to his heart. What was the worth of a man if his heart was empty? He thought of his life up to this point. The money. The privilege. The emptiness. And he suddenly knew the truth. "She didn't steal the idea, Nev. She wouldn't want the promotion if she had to get it that way."

Nev looked inordinately pleased with himself. "See, you didn't really lose at all today, now did you?"

As Eve had pointed out, he was creative and already an idea was forming. "Not yet, I haven't. I'd planned to leave the company if I lost this promotion, but I believe I've got to reconsider that." He couldn't contain the smile that had him grinning like an idiot. Or maybe just like a man in love. "I think I'd be foolish to miss the opportunity to work under a boss of Eve's caliber—unless there's a corporate policy against sleeping with the boss. And if that's the case, I'll need to contact a headhunter."

This time Nev looked inordinately pleased with Jack. "You know I'll miss you, Jack."

"How'd you know I'm moving?"

"Because Eve's in New York and I believe Jack LaRoux, now that he's discovered he has a heart, has decided to follow it."

"First thing tomorrow morning, I'll contact my boss and request a transfer to fill a recently vacated account position in the New York office."

"And what if she says no?"

"Well, if it's okay with you and Aunt Berta, I don't plan to lose again for a while."

EVE TOOK several deep breaths, oblivious to the cityscape outside the cab window. She'd never been so nervous before a presentation. Of course, she'd never had so much riding on a presentation. And she'd never been less sure of the outcome. But she was going to give it her best shot.

"This it, lady?" the driver asked.

With a start, Eve realized the cab had stopped. She paid the driver and forced herself to enter the building with a sure, confident stride.

The elevator whisked her to the fourth floor and she got off. A group of people, gathered around a coffeepot, eyed her with open interest.

She didn't stop however until she found who she was looking for. "Is he in?"

Neville turned around from his computer screen, a

sly smile tilting one corner of his mouth. "Hello. It's nice to finally meet you in person. Congratulations. I heard you were brilliant."

"I started that rumor," she said with a small smile, repeating the joke she'd shared with Neville before. Now that she was here, she was putting off going in to see Jack. "Aren't you surprised I'm here?"

"Not really."

Eve had only decided herself just in time to catch the last red-eye out. "How'd you know I'd come?"

"Woman's intuition." Nev dropped a conspiratorial wink.

Eve laughed. Neville was totally outrageous and she had a feeling they'd grow to be good friends.

"He's not here," Neville said, nodding toward the closed door.

Eve felt some of the wind go out of her sails. "Well, he's not in the office. He's in the building. Jack always gets in an early-morning swim and then works through lunch. The pool's on the first floor, left of the elevators. If you want to check it out."

"I'll do that."

Neville handed over a door card. "You'll need this to get in. And Jack always takes the stairs. Just so you won't miss him."

"Thanks, Neville."

"Don't mention it, Evil One."

Getting downstairs and to the workout room seemed to take forever.

The pool stood empty, but she hadn't passed Jack en route so he must be changing. She perched on the edge of a padded weight bench in the small workout room. The minutes dragged by until she spotted Jack leaving the dressing room, his hair still wet and slicked back. The instant she saw him, her nervousness vanished, replaced by the rightness of her decision. The rightness of the two of them.

Jack entered the workout room, obviously lost in thought.

She stood. "You missed a spot."

He pivoted on one foot to face her, shocked. "Eve? What?"

She closed the gap between them, grabbing a fresh towel off the stack by the machines. She dabbed the towel against his neck where his shirt gaped. "You missed a spot."

An uncertain smile curved his lips. "I bet you come with your very own warning label."

Eve laughed, dropping the towel. Jack always made her laugh. That was just one of the myriad things about this handsome, arrogant man that she loved to distraction. "Not that I'm aware of." Eve sobered. "Jack, we have unfinished business."

He squared his shoulders like a man awaiting sentencing. "I understand if you came to fire me before I could resign—"

"You think I would fly all the way to San Francisco to fire you?"

"I was a big enough jerk. I'd fly out here to fire me if I were you. But I hope you'll reconsider. What I'd really like to do is transfer to New York and fill your account position."

If he wanted her old position, that meant...joy blossomed inside her like a flower in the sun. "You want to work for me? Even though you think I stole your idea?"

Jack didn't wear sheepish well. "I owe you a tremendous apology. I know you didn't steal my idea."

"How could you possibly know that? What proof do you have?"

"All the proof I need. I finally listened to my heart. And if you can ever forgive me, if you'll have me..." Jack stopped. He wasn't supposed to stop just when he was getting to the good stuff. "If you didn't come to fire me, then why are you here, Eve?"

"To show you this." She pulled a typed, folded letter from her attaché.

Jack unfolded it and swiftly read it. But then again it was brief. He frowned. "This is a letter of resignation. Your resignation. Effective tomorrow."

Eve nodded.

"Why would you resign from a position that means so much to you?"

"Because you mean more. And I didn't know how else to prove to you that I didn't take the idea."

Jack scrubbed his hand through his hair, leaving it standing on end. "For God's sake, please tell me you haven't given a copy of this to Hendley yet."

"No, I took a personal day today and planned to give it to him tomorrow," she said. "I wanted to see you first."

"You'd do this for me? I mean this much to you?

You must be insane." He looked as if he couldn't quite assimilate it all.

She reached out and touched him, cupping his jaw, caressing his warm skin. "Not insane, just in love. But I think they're pretty much the same thing." She let her attaché case slide to the ground and wound her arms around his neck. "And I was willing to resign the position but I'm sure a headhunter could make it a lateral move so it's not as if I'm not giving up my career for you. Let's not overstate this."

Disbelief and cautious joy shone in his eyes. "Wait. Did you just mention that you love me?"

"Yes. I do love you, Jack." She pressed a kiss to his lips, imbuing it with all the love she felt for him.

"Then if you really love me, you'll tear up that resignation." Jack slid his arms around her waist and nuzzled her earlobe, his breath warm and arousing.

"Are you sure? You don't have any doubts about working for me?"

"I can handle you being on top, Eve. And no, I don't have any doubts." His gray eyes pierced hers, intense beneath his teasing tone, "I want a wife who's happy with her career."

"Wife?" The idea didn't frighten her nearly as much as it used to. Actually, it didn't frighten her at all.

"I told you from the beginning I didn't want to be your rival. I'm sure it won't always be easy, but I think we'll be much better collaborating with one another." He teased his lips against the corner of her mouth. "But we will have to check company policy about sleeping with the boss."

She pulled away. Jack's kisses tended to scatter her wits. "I think Hendley and Wells will be okay with it. If not we'll work something out."

"And a bigger apartment?"

"As long as you don't want to move to Hoboken."

"Consider it done. Eve?"

"Jack?"

"I know I'm a needy kind of guy, but tell me again why you wrote that resignation letter," he requested with a very satisfied smile.

She laughed up at him. "Because I finally found something that's better than chocolate."

The world's bestselling romance series.

HARLEQUIN®
Presents

Seduction and Passion Guaranteed!

THE PRINCESS BRIDES

For duty, for money…for passion!

Discover a thrilling new trilogy from a rising star of Harlequin
Presents®, Jane Porter!

Meet the Royals…

Chantal, Nicolette and Joelle are members of the blue-blooded
Ducasse family. Step inside their sophisticated and glamorous
world and watch as these beautiful princesses find they have
to marry three international playboys—for duty, for money…
and definitely for passion!

Don't miss

THE SULTAN'S BOUGHT BRIDE (#2418)
September 2004

THE GREEK'S ROYAL MISTRESS (#2424)
October 2004

THE ITALIAN'S VIRGIN PRINCESS (#2430)
November 2004

**Pick up a Harlequin Presents® novel and you will enter a world
of spine-tingling passion and provocative, tantalizing romance!**

Available wherever Harlequin books are sold.

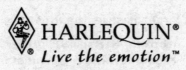

HARLEQUIN®
Live the emotion™

www.eHarlequin.com

HPPBJPOR

If you enjoyed what you just read,
then we've got an offer you can't resist!

Take 2 bestselling
love stories FREE!

Plus get a FREE surprise gift!